THE SAVAGE WAVES OF SPRING

Edited by David M. Olsen

Kelp Books, LLC

1491 Cypress Drive #475
Pebble Beach, Ca 93953

Copyright © 2026 Kelp Books, LLC All rights reserved

The characters and events portrayed in this book are fictitious. Any similarity to real persons, living or dead, is coincidental and not intended by the author.

No part of this book may be reproduced, or stored in a retrieval system, or transmitted in any form or by any means, electronic, mechanical, photocopying, recording, or otherwise, without express written permission of the publisher.

ISBN-13: 978-1-964880-10-5

Cover design by: Nusrat Design
Cover Painting by: OB Tune
Library of Congress Control Number: 2022949603
Printed in the United States of America

TABLE OF CONTENTS

Not Their Son 1
    by Curtis Ippolito

The Tarantulador 41
    by Jim Ruland

Wounded Things 61
    by C.W. Blackwell

The Coachella Death Pixie 83
    by Nik Xandir Wolf

The Spanish Shawl 93
    by Michael Scott Moore

Mrs. A 111
    by Kendall Brunson

Hitchhiker 133
    by Barbara DeMarco-Barrett

The Shadow of the Trough 153
    by Lindsay Jamieson

Imposter Syndrome 171
    by Joe Clifford

You Must Remember This 187
    by Gary Phillips

Heart of a Whale 219
    by Daniel Pyne

NOT THEIR SON

by Curtis Ippolito

Jerry Jensen knew his business partner Sunny had to be upset he was running so late. It was the only reason Sunny would've called his cell phone in the first place—three times while Jerry was out on his paddleboard.

He brought his 2004 GMC Sierra to a jerking stop in the gravel lot behind Sunny's Succulents, where they stored pallets of mulch, Sunny's homemade cactus soil, overstock plants, and where they loaded up landscape contractors. Sunny would be nailed to his regular spot, on that worn-out, backless rolling chair with no remaining seat cushion at the register.

Hustling to get there, Jerry cut through the main aisle that bisected the nursery. Morning dew had blanketed every plant with tiny droplets of moisture. The air smelled of a soothing combination of the nursery's organic matter and crisp salt water carried on the ocean breeze. He slipped past two of his employees—Brix and Kyle—gave them a nod. They waved in return. Kyle said, "Suh, Jerry."

When Jerry reached the register, he said, "So sorry I'm late, Sunny."

Sunny looked up from his coffee mug. A smile stretched across his wrinkled face.

"Don't sweat it," he said in the longtime-but-retired-smoker's voice of his. "Being late is kinda your whole deal, and as I keep telling you, your right as co-owner."

"I know, it's just—I'm way later than usual. Figured that's why you've been calling."

Sunny finished a sip of coffee, his long gray hair threatening to add some body to the brew. He set the mug down. "I wasn't checkin' up on you. I only called to give you a heads-up. Your wife's called three times already this morning looking for you."

As if on cue, the nursery's landline rang. Sunny picked up the cordless.

"If it's her, I'm still out on the water," Jerry said. "And it's *ex-wife*."

Sunny screwed his face, answered the call. "Sunny's Succulents, Sunny speaking. Uh-huh… Hi, again. Sorry, dear. Nothing's changed since you called. I'll make sure to let him know you're trying to reach him."

Jerry exhaled a breath he'd unconsciously been holding.

After hanging up, Sunny said, "She sounds worked up."

"Yeah… She's calling about Cody. He got arrested again, and I'm sure she wants me to do something about it."

"Hey, it's none of my business," Sunny said. "But maybe text her back so she'll stop gumming up the business line."

Jerry chuckled. "Sure. Wouldn't want to miss all of those important business calls."

Sunny snorted, smiled. Took another sip of his coffee.

"Any more of that?" Jerry asked. "Smells great."

"Yep. You know where."

"Great, thanks."

"Well," Sunny said, holding Jerry in place with the changing-subjects tone. "Did you namaste, or whatever, out there?"

Jerry laughed hard. For a child of the sixties who possessed all the physical characteristics of being the OG hippy Sunny was, it cracked Jerry up when his business partner didn't grasp tenets of mindfulness, chasing peace, and the like. "Namaste? I don't think you're using that right."

"Whatever."

"If you meant, did I have a chill session, then, no, not so much. The first half was pretty great. Then I had to save this knuckleheaded kid." Jerry raised his bandaged palms to Sunny.

Kyle jogged over, interrupting. "Hey." He swept the blond hair out of his eyes. "Should I water the two-inch succulents this morning?"

"Yes," said Sunny.

"But not the cactuses," Jerry added.

Kyle blinked, confused.

"They're the ones with spines," Jerry said.

"Gotcha!" Kyle shot them with finger guns and strolled off.

Jerry said to Sunny, "I've got to post those signs we made up."

"That'd be good." Sunny sipped his coffee. "You were saying something about saving a kid's life?"

Jerry motioned to follow him into the office–break room, which was little more than a lean-to connected to Sunny's crumbling bungalow. The room's roof leaked during winters when it actually rained in Southern California, and the walls consisted only of studs, no drywall.

Sunny was slow to get up, and the rolling chair creaked when he did. Various joints in his body popped when he took his first steps, prompting Jerry to turn his head and raise an eyebrow.

"Don't give me that look. You'll get old and frail one day too."

Jerry crossed the room. "You just need to move around a bit more." He removed a stainless steel cup out of the utility sink, gave it a quick rinse, filled it with hot coffee.

"Okay, whatever. Tell me about this kid already."

Jerry turned to him with big eyes. "Stupidest thing. A kid jumped off the cliff at the Cove, and I pulled him out. Spoiler: He lived."

Sunny followed Jerry out of the office and around the corner. They stopped at the Jerry-rigged shower, so nicknamed by the staff. Every morning, Jerry used the shower to rinse off after paddleboard sessions. He'd constructed it using a green garden hose run from a split-off under the sink in the office and bracketed to a cedar plank that was screwed to the lean-to. Jerry turned on the water, took a sip of his coffee, set it on the ground. He removed his shirt and handed it to Sunny. Jumping into the stream of frigid water, Jerry yelped.

"Glad the kid made it," Sunny said.

"Yeah, hopefully he won't do something that idiotic again." Jerry quick-rinsed and shut off the water. Grabbed a ratty towel hanging on a brass hook affixed to the lean-to and dried himself. "Man, have I had some morning."

"And you still have to call your wife."

"Ex-wife," Jerry said.

"Just talk to her, Jerry. Stop running away from your problems."

"Whoa, whoa. No need for violence so early." Jerry said.

* * *

Jerry retrieved his phone from his truck, saw Mia had called two more times and sent a few more texts since he'd last checked.

"I get it," he muttered, shoving the phone into his pocket. He lifted his paddleboard and paddle out of the truck bed and headed toward his place.

Cody, Jerry's son, had called him from jail two nights earlier and begged Jerry to bail him out. Jerry declined. Ever since, Mia had been blowing up his phone. He knew avoiding her wasn't going to work much longer.

Walking along the back property of the nursery, Jerry watched a few customers peruse the tables of small succulents. Emma, the nursery's only female employee, was helping them. Good kid.

Jerry heaved the board and paddle up against the side of the travel trailer Sunny had graciously allowed Jerry to make his home almost two years earlier. Sure, it leaked when it rained, stank of ancient ditch weed, and every piece of furniture inside was as worn out as Sunny's rolling chair. But it was home. It had other positives as well. A constant, cool breeze off the ocean just three blocks away, and it was free. Sunny's offer came at the perfect time, right when Jerry needed to get out of the house.

Leaning against the trailer, he selected missed calls on his phone, tapped *Mia*.

She picked up after one ring. "Jerry?"

"Hey, Mia. Guess you've been trying to get ahold of me?"

"Where have you been?"

"I was paddleboarding, then a teenager—"

"No," she said. "Where've you been the past two days? Cody's in jail, you know."

Jerry sighed. "Yeah. He called me."

Mia scoffed. And scoffed. Jerry needed to cut in or she might never stop.

"I told him that he's responsible for himself, and if he doesn't want to get arrested or spend any more time in jail in the future, he's the only one who can control that."

"Jesus. You can't bail out your only child to make things a little easier for him while we figure this out?"

Jerry paused. He wanted to simply tell her no, but he didn't want to deal with the fallout from that answer.

Instead, he said, "Why don't you bail him out yourself?"

"His bail is ten thousand dollars. I don't even have the thousand to pay the bond on that."

Jerry said nothing.

After a long pause: "I just want my boy home with me. He's not a bad person."

"I know that."

"So, why won't you help?"

Jerry didn't respond.

"Will you at least come over so we can talk about it in person?" she asked. "Please?"

Jerry could hear Mia stifling tears.

"So, I guess you're working nights these days?" he said.

"Yeah." She sniffed.

"Listen, I'll come over in an hour or so, but no promises beyond that."

"Okay. Thanks, Jerry."

"Sure."

* * *

Mia's old Honda Civic was parked in front of the house when Jerry arrived, so he killed his truck in front of the neighbor's house and walked up the sidewalk.

The front door and storm door were propped open. Music played from inside at a reasonable level. Duran Duran or The Cure—Jerry could never tell them apart. A vacuum ran in the distance. He knocked on the storm door and leaned inside the doorway.

"Mia?"

The vacuum shut off, and his ex-wife appeared, coming from down the hall. She wore cutoff jean shorts, a yellow Hurley shirt knotted at the waist, and white Skechers. Her brunette hair was pulled back in a bunch with loose strands framing her tan, slender face.

"Jerry!"

"Hey."

"Hey, yourself." Her cheeks flushed, and she cleared her throat. Reaching for the entry table, she tapped a cell phone and the music turned off.

"Cleaning?"

"Yeah, getting rid of some of Dad's things." She tucked the loose strands of hair behind her ears. "There's so much clutter."

Jerry stopped himself from saying "finally." He instead went with "uh-huh" and stuffed his hands in his back pockets.

"Do you...have a few minutes to help me?"

He shrugged. "Sure."

"Thanks, that would be a huge help. It's the newspapers." He knew immediately what she needed as she waved him inside.

His father-in-law's newspapers. Years and years of *The San Vista Gazette*. Piled up in mountains around his sagging, brown leather recliner, along the back of the couch, on one seat of the couch, blocking the fireplace, and along the walls. It was like a freaking newspaper archive in that room, and it constantly smelled like moldy newspaper and stale ink.

"I want to recycle them, but they won't all fit in my car. Could we load them in your truck and you drop them off for me?"

Jerry hesitated, wondered why she was suddenly so intent on cleaning up her late father's things five years after his passing.

"Sure," he said. Mia smiled. "I'll move my truck to the driveway, make it easier for us."

"Good idea."

On the walk to the truck, Jerry wondered if Mia was cleaning to distract herself from Cody's situation. Her father's mess had been one of the things they'd fought about when they were together. Jerry didn't say a word about it while the old man was alive—he had no right to, considering her father had allowed Jerry's family to move into his home when theirs was foreclosed on. Don, a Navy veteran, wasn't an easy nut to crack, but that didn't mean Jerry didn't respect the hell out of him, even despite his hoarding tendencies. Once he died though, Jerry couldn't understand why Mia hung on to his garbage.

Jerry backed his truck into the driveway, then moved things around in the bed to make room for the newspapers. He stacked empty plastic nursery pots together, pushed them up against the cab, and returned a rake, shovel, and pickaxe into slots in a rack anchored to one side of the bed.

Mia appeared with a stack of newspapers.

"Here," he said, holding out his arms. "I can take those."

"Thanks." She dropped the stack into his arms, and Jerry tossed them into the bed.

Dusting herself off, Mia said, "Did you bust up your hands working?"

"Oh, no. Just scratched them out on the water this morning."

She made a funny face.

He added, "On the reef."

"Ah, okay. Glad it's nothing serious. So, are you still doing gardening jobs?" She gestured with her head at the truck.

"Yeah. Held on to a few regulars to keep some money coming in until Sunny and I have things humming." Jerry motioned for them to go inside. She followed him.

"How long will that be?"

Jerry wrestled a large stack of newspapers from off the tower on the couch, jostling them to even them up in his arms. Mia followed him outside with her arms full as well. They heaved their hauls into the truck.

"He's doing the books, so it's hard for me to say for sure." Jerry clapped dust from his hands. "But I'm pretty sure we're only scraping by. Paying the vendors and the kids we've got working for us. Quality coffee is about the only thing that man spends money on."

Mia chuckled.

Hearing her laugh brought back memories of being able to make her bust out crying with laughter when they were younger. "I've got some things in the works that I hope will increase foot traffic and sales, but I can't throw too much change all at once at the old guy. I'm getting by okay, so I can't complain."

Mia nodded.

Neither said anything else. Jerry hooked a thumb toward the house.

Inside, silence grew between them. He didn't want to bring up Cody, but they needed to get it over with one way or another. He just wasn't looking forward to the inevitable shouting match. He grabbed more newspapers, clearing the remaining pile off the couch.

They fell into a good groove, hustling stacks of papers out to the truck. After not too long, they vanquished the wall of newspapers against the back of the couch and put a significant dent in the piles around the recliner and fireplace.

The bed of the truck was filling up, a mound forming.

Having lapped Mia at some point, Jerry came out to the truck on one trip to find her holding a newspaper open, smiling.

"What's that?" he asked.

"You remember that summer when Cody was twelve and he was so excited for that scout trip to the national forest?"

Jerry did. He had looked forward to it, too. He volunteered to chaperone, recognizing the trip as a chance to spend some time with his quickly growing son. To ensure he could go, Jerry worked from four in the morning to nine at night—mowing and blowing back then—all that week to free up his weekend.

"Yeah, I remember."

"The Santos Fire. That was a bad one." Mia pursed her lips and folded up the paper. "Cody was so disappointed that trip got canceled."

"Yeah, me too." Jerry tossed his pile of newspapers into the truck. "He didn't want to do anything else either. Just stayed in his room the entire weekend, pouting."

"Could you blame him?"

"No. Bummed me out, too."

Mia smiled. "You're a good dad." She brushed his shoulder as she headed up the front walk to the house. Jerry didn't reply. Was she being sincere? Or sweet-talking him for when she would put the full-court press on him to bail out Cody?

Jerry met her inside, unsure if he should say something or if the moment had passed. He always strived to be a good dad to Cody, better than the parents who'd run off on him when he was a kid. Trying to shake the thought, Jerry said, "We've almost got this place cleared out."

"Uh-huh." Mia didn't look at him.

"*The San Vista Gazette.* Haven't read an actual print copy in years. You?"

"The clinic gets a copy every day," she said, turning around with arms full. "Some of the doctors still prefer the print version. I flip through it when I'm on lunch if I haven't already read the news online."

"Yeah, I get my news secondhand from Sunny. Whether I want to hear it or not." Jerry scooped up the last of the newspapers along the wall, a stack about half of what they'd been carrying out.

After tossing the newspapers in the truck, Jerry closed the tailgate and retrieved a set of red tie straps from the cab. Together, they crisscrossed the straps over the massive pile of newspapers, secured the hooks to the truck, and Jerry ratcheted the straps down tight.

"She's not going anywhere," he said.

Mia stood in the grass. "Thanks again. This is a huge help."

"Sure." Jerry clapped his hands on his shorts.

She smiled. Took a short breath, hesitating to say something. "I know you believe in the tough love approach with Cody, and I'm not going to argue that with you again."

"Okay…"

"But he's scared, Jerry. He wants to come home. Is it so wrong to want to get him out? He'll still have to answer for his actions, even if they arrested him on BS this time."

"BS?" Jerry said. "How is stealing watches off tourists bullshit, Mia?"

"It was a misunderstanding."

"Oh, sure." Jerry threw up his hands. "I'm sure the watches magically fell off those tourists' wrists or got left somewhere or were lost, and Cody just happened to come along and find them and was on his way to take them to lost and found when he got caught."

Mia huffed, crossed her arms. "That's not the point. Why can't you help get him out while we figure out the next steps?"

Jerry felt his neck get hot. "Even if I wanted to, I don't have the money to risk on bailing him out."

"Well, I don't have the money period."

"Aren't you making more now as an RN?"

"I'm not an RN yet. I'm still taking the classes, which is why I'm broke."

"I thought work was paying for your tuition."

"Not until I finish. It's a tuition reimbursement program. I maxed out my credit cards paying for the classes."

She flopped her arms to her side. She looked as exasperated as she sounded.

Jerry fidgeted with the tailgate handle, avoiding her eyes.

"And by the way, you wouldn't be *risking* your money," Mia said. "He's your son."

"Sorry. I didn't mean it like that. It's the principle. He did something wrong. I can't—"

"How about this?" Mia stepped closer to him. "Will you at least go by and see him in person before you decide not to help him?"

"Why?"

"To tell him to his face that you won't bail him out."

Jerry groaned.

"You can do that at least, right?"

Jerry inhaled deeply through his nose, felt his chest rise. He had never visited Cody in the twenty-two months he was in county jail, and always felt shitty about it. He'd only seen him twice in the year since he'd been out, too.

"Yeah. I guess I can do that… I'll try to go by tomorrow."

Mia jumped at him and hugged him. "Thank you!"

"No promises though."

She squeezed him tighter. And for the first time in years, he didn't pull away from her.

* * *

The closest beach access to Jerry's trailer and Sunny's Succulents was a four-block walk away. A semi-private entrance at the end of a cul-de-sac—sandwiched between monstrous Spanish Colonials—that you had to know was there to find it. Meaning, Cipher's Beach fifty-four concrete steps below inevitably retained a distinctive locals-only vibe, with surfers who ferociously protected its reputation. Even though Jerry told anyone who asked why he drove five miles south to paddleboard at the Cove that it was because the water there was consistently calmer, Cipher's locals-only attitude was the real reason. It bugged the ever-loving crap out of him that anyone would have the stones to patrol the open water and make it their business as to who was and wasn't welcome to catch a wave.

So, like every day, he street parked at the Cove early morning. The sunrise painted everything with a pink glow—from the sleek luxury vehicles and beachside mansions to the smooth asphalt streets and meticulously maintained sidewalks.

With two forceful tugs, Jerry unloaded his SUP from his truck bed. Not a second later, his phone rang from inside the cab. Mia. Had to be.

Two days earlier, Jerry had blown off going to see Cody in jail. She'd apparently figured that out and was calling him to read him the riot act.

Jerry propped the board against the tailgate and waited for the ringing to stop before snatching the paddle from the bed. After opening the back door, he tossed his flip-flops on the floorboard. Next, he shed his shirt.

His phone started ringing again. She wouldn't stop. But why should he care? He'd be on the water in thirty seconds and wouldn't hear it anymore. *Yeah, but*, said a voice inside his head. He would hear *it* when he came back and finally returned her calls.

Jerry opened the truck and grabbed the phone. Answering, Mia said, "Jerry? Jerry, are you there?" her voice frantic.

"Hey, Mia. I was just about to get on the water—"

"The lawyer called. You have to meet me at the jail right now." She talked so fast some of her words ran together.

"Lawyer? What lawyer?"

"I hired a lawyer for Cody. How soon can you get here?"

Jerry heard the urgency in her tone, even if he couldn't piece together what she was telling him. "What happened now?"

"Cody's got a new charge!"

"A new charge?" None of this was making any sense to Jerry. Their son hadn't moved from jail in days. It was the very point of contention between him and Mia. So how could Cody have a new charge against him? "He get into a fight or something?"

Mia's voice cracked. She gulped a breath of air before speaking again.

"He's been charged with trafficking a minor, Jerry." She burst into tears.

Jerry felt like he was falling backward. He looked around, shocked, confused.

Trafficking a minor? What the hell?

"Mia." He pinned the phone against his ear with his shoulder, threw his board and paddle back in the bed, then climbed into the truck. Hands shaking, he buckled his seat belt. "I'll be there as soon as I can."

* * *

Jerry found parking easy enough at the men's jail, a feat never to be taken for granted anywhere in downtown San Vista, no matter the time of day. Finding the entrance for visitations was a little trickier. After trying one entrance, he was informed visitations was actually on the other side of the ten-story building.

The walk around gave him time to try to process what was going on with his son. Ever since Cody had started acting out as a young teen, he'd only ever gotten in trouble for crimes of theft. But trafficking a minor? What the hell? Not his son. It seemed way out of Cody's character to be involved with prostitution, much less trafficking a child. Entertaining that possibility turned Jerry's stomach.

When he entered, Mia was pacing the lobby's green linoleum floor.

"Jerry. C'mon." She clapped her hands, then pointed to a female sheriff's deputy sitting behind plexiglass. "Get checked in."

"Good to see you, too."

She ignored him.

After he signed the visitor log, relinquished his phone and keys, they were buzzed in. Jerry held open the heavy iron door for her, and a beefy guard with a death stare met them on the other side. He escorted Jerry and Mia down a long, beige hallway to a vast, windowless room. It was brisk inside. Jerry wished he was wearing more than board shorts, a T-shirt, and flip-flops.

"Sit here," said the guard, motioning to one of the many metal tables in the space. "We'll bring him out soon."

"Thank you," Jerry said. He took a seat on one of the frigid aluminum stools that were bolted down around the table. Mia sat to his right. He turned to her, leaned in. "What the hell is going on?"

With her forehead wrinkled and green eyes glassier than the Cove on its stillest day, she said, "All I know is the DA charged him with trafficking a minor."

"Jesus Christ... How could he traffic anything while he's locked up?"

"That doesn't make sense to me either. The lawyer is meeting us here, so hopefully he can fill us in."

Jerry eased away, sat up. He wanted to ask her how she'd been able to pay for a lawyer when she had begged him to cover Cody's bail, no doubt the less expensive proposition of the two. But such a question felt accusatory, out of bounds. A question their divorce disallowed as sure as it split them apart permanently.

Mia wrung her hands. "He's a good lawyer." She said it quietly, as if trying to convince herself.

"Did you take out a loan or something to hire him?" Jerry couldn't help himself. Cody was his kid, too, after all.

"Yes," she said.

He realized something a second later. "Is that why you were cleaning out the house?"

"Yes. I got a home equity loan." She pushed loose strands of hair behind her ears. "What else could I do?"

Jerry couldn't fault her for going all out to hire a good lawyer this time around. They'd been down this road before. Cody's defense last trial had fallen to a public defender, who did a decent enough job, considering. He'd arranged a plea deal that shaved years off what a potential guilty verdict would've handed down. But Mia hadn't wanted Cody to plead guilty. So, Mia hiring a lawyer this time made sense. She wasn't leaving Cody's fate to whether he drew a good PD or not. That had to be her thinking.

As it was, the robbery charge that locked up their son this time was a dot in the rearview mirror now, compared to the trafficking charge barreling its way at them.

"Do we know how much his bail is now?"

"No." Mia rubbed her palms on her jeans. "I'm nervous for him, Jerry. He's a good boy. He shouldn't be back in here."

Jerry said nothing. He did feel compelled to comfort her, though, so he rested his hand on her shoulder for a few seconds. Then folded his hands and flopped them in his lap.

The two sat in silence, each lost in their own world.

Five minutes later, a door at the opposite side of the room opened.

"Cody!" Mia jumped to her feet. Tears erupted, streamed down her cheeks.

Jerry stood slowly.

A male guard escorted Cody to the table. "Thirty minutes. No touching."

"Thank you," said Jerry and Mia simultaneously.

"Hi, Mom." Cody smiled at her. She reached out, touched his hands—secured in handcuffs—before pulling back quickly to avoid being reprimanded. Cody nodded. "Dad."

"Son."

The Jensens all sat down. Jerry couldn't remember the last time they'd shared a table together. Had to be before Cody's jail sentence. More than four years ago at this point.

"What's going on?" Jerry said. "Did you really traffic a minor?"

Mia jumped in before Cody could respond. "Are they treating you well? Are you eating? You look pale."

"I'm fine, Mom."

But he looked pretty pale to Jerry, too. His skin was practically translucent in contrast to his dark brown, shoulder-length hair. His eyes were sunken in their sockets. Blue blood vessels were clearly visible, running from his skinny wrists up to his nonexistent biceps, where the oversized sleeves of his tan jumper took over.

"Cody," Jerry said firmly. "What's going on?"

"Hey, Dad. Glad you could finally come see me." Gesturing with his hands, Cody droned, "Welcome to the lovely San Vista Men's Downtown Jail, home to an average population of nine hundred inmates—"

"Stop it," Jerry said. "And I didn't put you in here. You did that to yourself."

"Jerry." Mia said his name curtly while landing an elbow into his ribs.

He grimaced. "Sorry."

Several long seconds passed.

Cody dropped his head. "I'm sorry, too." He stared at his lap and took a deep breath. "I have no idea what's going on. I didn't do anything. I've been in here for four days, so how could I pimp a prostitute, or whatever the hell they're calling it?" He looked at them with his big, brown eyes. "Honest. I'm as confused as you are."

Hearing his son speak, Jerry questioned his skepticism of Cody's new charge. Cody played innocent victim better than anyone. He never did anything wrong... He didn't steal those packages off porches when he was twelve. Wasn't the one who stole the Shriners Hospital for Children donation containers filled with bills and loose change from twelve different convenience stores later the same year. He certainly didn't jack the neighbor's Altima when he was fifteen and drive it up the coast until he got bored of the joyride and nosed it into a protected lagoon. No, never. Not him...

"Guess we'll see what the lawyer says," Jerry said.

Mia said, "We believe you, baby. We'll get you out of here if we can."

Jerry sat back, folded his arms. He watched Mia lean across the table, trying to get as close to Cody as the guards would allow. The two of them started up about what he was eating, reading, doing to keep his mind off being there again. They fell into an intimate back-and-forth, like they were the only two in the room. The way they did when Cody was a child. Every night, Mia would tuck him in and Jerry would watch from the doorway. Watching them back then, he always found himself smiling, happy they had a tight bond. Proud of the fact that his son would never be shuttled from one family member to the next, abandoned by his parents like Jerry had been. But as happy as he felt in those moments, over time Jerry became envious of Mia and Cody's connection, which inevitably led to him feeling like a grade A shit heel. Then, in Cody's adolescence, his and Mia's relationship transitioned. She'd constantly alibi for his bad decisions. That's when the wedge widened between wife and husband. She always took Cody's side, and so, in Jerry's mind, she had enabled their son's criminal bent.

Footsteps echoed in the room. Jerry turned around to see a Black man around his same age, dressed in a suit, headed their way. "Lawyer is here."

Mia jumped out of her seat, ran over to him, and thrust her hand at him. He shook it.

"Please. Tell us what's going on," she pleaded.

"Of course. Let me get introductions out of the way first." He sat down to the right of Mia. Making eye contact with Cody, he said, "My name is Donald Anderson, and I will be representing you."

"Cool," Cody said. "Are you getting me out of here?"

"Well, not exactly. Your initial bail has since been increased. Which is why I am here—to explain to you why and what is happening. From there, it will be up to your family to cover your bond if you're to be released, awaiting trial."

Jerry leaned across the table to see past Mia. The lawyer continued.

"The district attorney has submitted a charge of human trafficking of a minor, which carries a potential sentence of ten years."

Mia covered her mouth. Jerry shook his head.

Cody said, "What the hell? I didn't do shit."

"The DA says it ascertained evidence of you directing an underaged female to engage in sexual acts with an adult male for the exchange of money, and then you requested this underage female use the money to bail you out of jail," Anderson said.

Cody stamped his feet and slammed his fists on the table. Defiance etched on his face.

"Is that true, Cody?" Mia said. He didn't reply and avoided eye contact. "Cody?"

He huffed, looked at her. "No. I swear."

Jerry said, "What's the evidence the DA has?"

The lawyer took a deep breath and gave Cody a glance before giving his full attention to Jerry. "They have a recorded phone call between Cody and the underaged female in question, and then video of their visit here in jail, with clear audio of him making the request."

Cody scoffed. Fidgeted in his seat. "I mean, yeah. I called a friend to ask her to help me." Pointing at Jerry, he added, "You told Mom you were coming to bail me out, and you never came. I didn't know what else to do."

"I didn't say I would bail you out, only hear you out—"

"But you didn't come, and I can't be in here anymore. I just can't," Cody said.

"So you pimped out a child?" Jerry shouted.

"Shut up!" Cody ducked, scanned the room. "No. I mean… She's not a child, she's my friend. She's a sex worker, and yes, she's seventeen. But I never asked her to have sex with anyone. Only to get some money from one of her rich clients."

"So you blackmailed someone?"

"No! It wasn't like that."

Mia said, "Okay, okay," and physically got between the two of them. "Calm down, both of you." Once Jerry and Cody settled down, she turned to the lawyer. "How bad is it?"

"It's not good. I'm waiting to see the video and hear the audio, but if it's as incriminating as the DA says, it's going to be an uphill battle."

"Fantastic," Cody said.

"Plus," Anderson added, "they said the john is cooperating. Apparently, he has already confirmed that the underaged female propositioned him on Cody's directions and attempted to blackmail him."

"This is such bullshit. She's my friend. We grew up together."

"Who is she, sweetheart?" Mia asked.

"Juliana Gomez. Remember her?"

"Sure," Mia said. "Her family lived across from us on Spring Ravine, before we moved in with Grandpa."

The name clicked with Jerry. Sweet Mexican girl, a little younger than Cody, who was always at their house playing with a couple of other kids from the neighborhood.

"I will try to contact her and see if she will cooperate with us," said Anderson. "But if she is facing charges of her own, she might not want to help."

"What about the bond?" Mia asked. "How much is it now?"

"Fifty thousand dollars," said Anderson. "You'll need to come up with ten percent—five thousand dollars—in addition to putting up something of value, such as a house, as collateral."

"Time's up," said a guard, appearing out of nowhere and standing at the end of the table.

"Already?" Cody said. The guard didn't respond.

Mia stood. "Cody, honey. Take care of yourself. We'll be sending you positive thoughts."

"You're getting me out here though, right?"

"Time," the guard said more forcefully.

Mia shot a look at Jerry, and then back at Cody. "We'll do our best. Love you, baby."

"You, too, Mom."

"Be good, Cody," Jerry said.

* * *

Jerry and Mia agreed to meet at A1 Bonds, adjacent to the downtown men's jail where their son was being held. When Jerry told her he would pay to bail out Cody, Mia had hugged him tighter than he could remember.

In only a few days, Jerry had gone from dug in, refusing to reward Cody's criminality by bailing him out of jail, to now believing his son was likely wrapped up in the middle of something deviant, or at the very least, unjust. Cody deserved to be free while his lawyer worked to prove his innocence. Jerry shook his head. He could've saved himself $4,000 if he had simply agreed to bail him out when he was first arrested. Not to mention, Cody wouldn't have been desperate enough to call on a friend to squeeze money out of a rich creep and put himself in this position to begin with.

As Jerry looked for a place out front to lean against, Mia jogged around the corner.

"Why haven't you got started?" she said. Jerry held the door open for her.

"Figured they need you here, too, for the collateral part. You okay putting up the house?"

She shot him a "Do you even have to ask?" look.

"Can I help you folks?" The question came from a regular-looking guy who wore a company polo and khaki pants.

"Here to bond out our son, Cody Jensen. J-e-n-s-e-n."

"Cody Jensen. Let me look him up."

Mia smiled at Jerry and rubbed his back like she used to after a long workday back when they were still together. His ears warmed. The small touches of intimacy were what he missed most about being with her. Even at their most strapped—finances a wreck, no clear idea how their income would cover everything—she always made an effort to ease his stress with neck rubs, a warm hug, or by running her hand through his hair. In the early years, that is.

"Sorry, looks like his bail has been canceled," said the employee.

"What?" Mia said.

"How's that possible?" Jerry added.

"The system doesn't tell me that. Just says bail has been canceled by order of Judge William Sparks."

Mia slammed her palm on the counter. "No! That's not possible. We just saw our son's lawyer ten minutes ago and he gave us the amount."

"Sorry, ma'am."

"Is there anything we can do?" Jerry asked.

The employee shrugged. "Talk to your lawyer?"

* * *

Donald Anderson's law office was a mile outside of downtown, inside a creaky, pink Victorian home that also housed three additional tenants.

Mia and Jerry sat in padded office chairs at Anderson's desk, each looking around as they waited impatiently for his arrival. He'd been curt with them when they called his cell, said he was on the other line with the DA.

"Kinda weird his office used to be a bedroom," Jerry said.

Mia didn't respond. Instead, she stared out one of the windows to their right. Disappointment surrounded her like an aura. Her silence felt like a boat anchor slung around Jerry's neck that got heavier with each passing second.

Why hadn't he bailed out Cody when he'd called from jail? Or when Mia pleaded with Jerry to? Was he so infatuated with thinking the law could teach Cody some kind of lesson that he would allow his only son to rot in a cell? If only Jerry would have listened to Mia, none of this would be happening.

The floor creaked behind them. Both jolted, turned around. It wasn't Anderson, however, but Kaili, his energetic administrative assistant, standing in the doorway.

"Can I get either of you a sparkling water or tea or something?" she asked. Her positivity stood in sharp contrast to the mood of the room.

Mia turned back to the window. "No, thank you."

"A water would be nice," Jerry said.

"Coming right up, Mr. Jensen." Kaili bounded away.

Jerry straightened in his chair. "Mia, I'm sorry I didn't listen to you sooner." He paused, thinking he heard a hitch in her breathing, like she was about to say something. But she didn't.

"Good afternoon, Mr. and Mrs. Jensen." Anderson entered the office, his demeanor neither chipper nor sullen. "I have come from seeing Cody and informing him of the latest developments in his case."

"How did he take it?" Mia asked.

"He was very upset, understandably."

"What the hell is going on?" Jerry asked.

Anderson settled in his desk chair. Leaned forward and rested his elbows on the desk, intertwining his fingers. "I'm sorry you had to find out the way you did. It all happened so fast. As you discovered, Cody's bail has been canceled. Judge Sparks made the decision after the DA filed four additional charges of human trafficking of a minor against Cody, as well as a charge of extortion."

Mia and Jerry simultaneously exclaimed, "What?"

"I know this is a shock. Allow me to fill you in completely. The DA petitioned the court to cancel Cody's bail in light of the new charges, arguing if he were to bond out, he could pose a flight risk, living in such close proximity to the border."

"That's ridiculous. Cody wouldn't run," Mia said.

"During the course of its investigation of Cody's jailhouse call and visitation with his accomplice, and interviewing the witness who says he was targeted by Cody and his accomplice, the DA received information of four additional times when, the witness alleges, Cody supplied him with underage sex workers."

"That's ridiculous," Jerry said.

Mia shook her head vehemently. "Cody would never!"

Anderson continued. "The DA is giving the witness immunity in exchange for his testimony against Cody at trial."

"What?" Mia shouted.

"Wait," Jerry said. "So, the guy who actually had sex with these minors is going to get off scot-free for sending our son up the river? How does that make any sense?"

Kaili entered the office then and placed a bottle of water in front of Jerry, then slunk out.

"I know this is upsetting news," Anderson said. "Unfortunately for Cody, California law prioritizes punishing the pimp over the sex buyer."

Mia scoffed. "Pimp?"

"I am sorry, Mrs. Jensen. At this point in time, the state believes your son is a pimp. The state also believes it can reduce underage prostitution more effectively by cutting off the supplier of underage sex workers rather than going after every sex buyer."

"This makes no sense at all to me," Jerry said.

"And I understand that," Anderson said. "It is confusing and does seem counterintuitive, but these are the realities of the law at the present time."

Mia and Jerry fell back in their chairs. Gave each other a "What the hell?" look before turning their attention to Anderson again.

"So, what can we do?" Mia asked.

Anderson took a breath. "I had another case a few months ago similar to Cody's. A young man a few years older than Cody. He was busted in a sting providing underage prostitutes to several sex buyers at a hotel. The DA declined to charge the buyers with anything and went after my client. Long story short, he is now serving a twenty-year sentence with parole not possible until 2037. The DA is taking these cases seriously. With that said, I believe our best option for Cody is to seek a plea deal in the hope of lessening his potential sentence."

"All due respect," Jerry said, "that case doesn't sound like Cody's at all. Your guy sounds like he was an actual pimp. Our son's been in a jail cell through all of this."

"They are difficult to compare," Anderson said. "But I can assure you the parallels are there, and the DA isn't focused on nuance. It will be extremely difficult to prove Cody's innocence up against the testimony of the DA's witness."

"What are you saying?" Jerry asked.

"Basically, the DA is more likely to believe the account of a prominent member of the San Vista community over a young man with a criminal record," Anderson said. "In any event, Cody gave me the phone number of Juliana, the girl in question. I will follow up with her, but in the meantime, I strongly advise you not to make contact with her, or anyone else involved in this case besides your son."

"I can't lose Cody to jail again," Mia said.

"Prison is more like it," Jerry said. The lawyer nodded. Jerry continued, "And a sentence for trafficking children? We might as well plan his funeral right now. No way our scrawny boy lasts a year with that rap hanging over his head. And when it should be the true pervert instead? Prominent community member, my ass. This is so messed up."

"I understand your concerns. I can request a minimum security facility and a solitary cell for Cody," Anderson said. "No guarantees, but we can raise our concerns about his safety."

Jerry felt the momentum of the conversation pulling in one direction. Toward a plea deal. This lawyer wanted the easy way out, to be done with this loser case.

Jerry asked, "What else can we do? Anything? You said the DA favors their witness's testimony over Cody's. Can anything change his mind?"

"Not right now. We can give it some time, though. We'll have the criminal grand jury next, then the judge will set a date for the trial. Let's see how things play out over the next few weeks, but short of the witness getting caught doing the same thing or worse that he's blaming Cody for, the chances the DA sticks to the deal they have with their witness is a lock."

"This is wrong!" Jerry slammed a fist on the desk. Mia laid a hand on his shoulder. Tears ran down her cheeks.

Kaili darted into the room. Anderson ushered her away with a sincere look, a shake of the head, and a palm extended.

"I am truly sorry I was unable to deliver better news, Mr. and Mrs. Jensen."

Jerry stood. He wanted to throw his chair through one of the windows. Instead, he wrapped an arm around Mia and guided her out of the office.

Once outside, they walked to their cars in silence.

Mia blotted tears with her scrub top. Jerry started to say something, but a commercial plane flew overhead on its final descent, so he paused. Once clear, he said, "I'll check in on you tomorrow."

Mia gave a slight nod, got in her Civic and drove away.

* * *

Jerry straddled his paddleboard—legs dipped in the ocean to his knees, body pointed at the endless horizon. The water was a perfect 60 degrees, while the sun hadn't yet grown strong enough to warm his back. Not so much as a ripple across the ocean's surface as far as the eye could see.

These were all merely facts to Jerry, though. Nothing he noted beyond such. The perfect day for an SUP session, and instead of enjoying it, Jerry fumed.

It had been a week since he and Mia met with Cody's lawyer and learned of the new charges against their son. In that time, a criminal grand jury had heard the charges and returned an indictment against Cody. A trial date was set for three months from now. Three months for Cody to sit in his jail cell with nothing to do to improve his situation. Jerry didn't even want to think of how his son would be treated once word spread through the jail of the new charges against him. Donald Anderson had said the DA didn't see nuance in these kinds of cases, and Jerry assumed the same held true for inmates. Trafficking minors would be all they'd hear. Cody's innocence be damned.

Anderson hadn't been able to reach Cody's friend Juliana, either. He drove out to her grandmother's place in addition to dozens of calls and voicemails left. Nothing. She was in the wind. No help to Cody. Fending for herself. No one could blame her.

During one of the proceedings, the DA's witness appeared in court. Edwin Rosten was his name. One of those retired software tycoons. Dressed to the nines. Black suit and tie, wing tips that reflected every light in the courtroom. Jerry wanted to throw him against a wall. See fear in the eyes of that piece of shit, hear exactly why he was selling out their son.

Because he can.

That's what Mia had said later that night after meeting with Anderson. Jerry had called to check on her after he'd downed a six-pack of Stone beers back at his trailer. She sounded a world and a half away. Tired. Wrung out. While Jerry had run away and tried to ignore Cody's trouble with the law and being sent to jail for eighteen months, Mia stuck by her son. She saw the good in him like only a mother could.

Jerry raised his paddle above his head and brought it down swiftly, slapping the water to his right. The board rocked.

After that night, he and Mia had gone to visit Cody the next day. Mia tried to smile and remain positive, even though her puffy eyes gave away her true emotions. Cody didn't say much. Neither did Jerry. What was there to say? None of them made eye contact with each other, but Jerry stole looks of his son. His eyes were sunken with dark pockets underneath like he wasn't getting sleep. How could he? Cody kept cracking his knuckles, even after they'd popped all they could. Above each knuckle on his hand, tattooed emblems of the four suits of cards. From pointer finger to pinkie ran spades, diamonds, hearts, clubs. Both hands. Got them when he was sixteen. Mia was disappointed, and Jerry livid. Cody said he was going to be a card shark, but he turned out to be a shit cardplayer, just like his old man.

When their visitation time was up, Jerry wanted to apologize to Cody, tell him he should have bailed him out when he'd asked. But his tongue felt fat. He couldn't spit out the words. Nothing he could've said then would've done much good anyway.

Jerry maneuvered his board to the south. He now faced the direction of downtown. Where he'd discovered Edwin lived. He wondered how long it would take to paddle there. Probably an hour or two, but he thought he could do it. He'd worked up the stamina with his daily sessions. God, how great would it feel to pay Edwin a surprise visit and punch him square in his fat nose a few dozen times?

In fact, Jerry had been having a recurring dream about doing that exact thing.

Jerry plopped back down on his ass.

His ears burned hot. He could feel the veins in his neck throbbing.

He let the paddle slide through his hands until he gripped the end like a baseball bat. Loading the paddle over his head, he smacked the hell out of the surface of the ocean. Over and over and over again.

* * *

It took three days for Jerry to catch a glimpse of Edwin Rosten.

After wrestling with what to do on his paddleboard that morning, Jerry decided to feed his anger. Confront Edwin. Get him to recant his testimony. If needed, he'd beat a conscience into him. Sunny didn't ask Jerry where he was all day, and Jerry didn't offer. Better to keep his business partner in the dark for the time being.

Same went for Mia.

The first two days, Jerry sat in his truck out front of Edwin's condominium building. Packed PB and J sandwiches and a large thermos of coffee kept him fed and awake. Turned out the coffee was critical, as hour after hour passed without spotting Edwin.

Maybe Jerry needed to get there earlier or stay later to see him come or go? Maybe Edwin had another home, was there instead. People with his wealth always had additional residences, right?

Jerry chipped away at the possibilities.

On the third day, he showed at five a.m. Still nothing. While waiting, he did some research on his phone to see if Edwin had another home. He searched "Edwin Rosten home address" and "Edwin Rosten address San Vista" and several other combinations using the names of different affluent neighborhoods but came up with nothing.

Around three p.m., Jerry found himself bored, losing hope. He got out of his truck and found an alley to relieve himself. After finishing and zipping up, Jerry trudged back. Ran his hand down the side of his truck. That's when he heard dress shoes knocking hard against concrete. Looking across the street, he saw Edwin exiting the condo's underground parking garage. Dressed in a pressed white shirt, navy slacks and wearing aviator sunglasses, heading into the building. How the hell had he gotten past Jerry in the first place? Didn't matter.

Jerry hustled across the street and slipped into the building behind Edwin. Inside, Edwin strutted to the bank of elevators, passing a desked guard without a word or a wave. To Edwin's credit, the guard had his face buried in his phone, which allowed Jerry to sneak to the elevators and jump inside the elevator with Edwin. Keeping his head down, he moved to the opposite side,

Edwin unaware, now also on his phone, talking in a gruff tone under his breath.

In no time, the elevator dinged. They'd reached the penthouse floor.

Jerry's heart hammered in his chest. Beads of sweat streamed down his temples.

Edwin ended his call and got off while Jerry lingered inside. As the doors began to close, Jerry thrust out his arm, and the doors reopened. Getting off, he waited for Edwin to reach the end of the hall, approach his front door. Edwin extended his arm. A clicking noise sounded.

Jerry bolted down the hallway. Before he could reach the condo, however, a slight figure—a woman—jumped in front of him from out of nowhere and rushed Edwin.

"Inside!" she said.

Edwin startled, threw up his hands.

Shocked, Jerry said, "Mia?" She didn't react, only kept her attention on Edwin. It was then that Jerry saw she had a gun—pointed at Edwin.

She left the door open. Jerry followed them inside the condo. After he quietly closed the door, he watched Mia back Edwin into his living room. A spacious area with white leather couches, matching shag area rugs, and floor-to-ceiling views of the glistening San Vista Bay.

"What are you doing, Mia?" Jerry asked.

"Yes. What are you doing, dear?" sneered Edwin. Jerry saw he wasn't worried in the slightest. The DA's star witness against their son casually removed his aviators, set them on a glass table.

He ran his hands through an obviously plug-enhanced and dyed mop of black hair.

"Don't call me 'dear,' you sick piece of shit."

Jerry had never seen her like this. He thought she'd been reeling, yet she embodied confidence in her actions. Actions that had taken time or rage to plan, or both.

"What are *you* doing here, Jerry?" she said over her shoulder.

"Same as you. Came to talk some sense into him."

At this, Edwin barked out a laugh. "You two must be fresh off the boat if you think I'm going to do anything to jeopardize my freedom."

"Shut the hell up!" Mia shouted. "And no, Jerry. I'm not here to talk. I'm here to *do* something about this. I'm done letting the world get one over us just because we're not rich and connected. My son is a good boy." She kept her distance from Edwin, like he was too poisonous to get close to. Keeping her distance also had the advantage of keeping him from being able to grab the gun. "He's made a few mistakes, but nothing like the shit you're pinning on him."

"So, what? You're going to kill me?" Edwin asked.

Mia didn't answer, just kept her eyes drilled into Edwin.

Jerry said, "Mia. This isn't you. Let me handle this."

"No, Jerry. You handling it has made everything worse. I'm sick of you running away from problems and leaving me to clean them up. But I do it. It's what I've always done. Clean up messes and fix people."

"That's right," Jerry said. "You heal people. That's what you do. You're a nurse. You don't kill people."

Mia scowled. But she kept the gun on Edwin.

Jerry touched her elbow, careful not to startle her. "Will you at least talk to me first?"

"Hey!" she yelled, thrusting the gun at Edwin, who was slipping a hand into his pocket. "Go ahead, pull out that phone, but slow. Good. Now put it on the table with your sunglasses."

"You've watched too many movies, nurse."

"Shut up," she said. "Hands on your head." Edwin sighed but complied.

Jerry touched Mia's elbow again, and she jerked away. Then, she took two or three steps backward, not dropping the gun even a centimeter.

"What?"

Getting close, Jerry whispered, "What's your plan here?" He heard her stop breathing, then begin again, controlled. Slow and measured.

"Same as you. Convince him to take back his testimony. I can't physically dominate him, so, the gun."

"Okay. So, give me the gun. I'll—"

"No, Jerry!" She took focus off Edwin for a split second to give Jerry a look of derision. "No." She lowered her voice again. "I'll keep the gun on him, and you talk. Let's work together for once."

With that, she stepped forward and aimed the gun with purpose at Edwin's chest.

"Don't do this, please." Edwin's tone now pleading. Finally realizing fear. Maybe for the first time ever.

This could work, Jerry thought.

Edwin had scurried back to the window and cowered there.

Mia stepped forward to close the distance but tripped on the edge of one of the shag rugs. The gun went off.

Jerry's ears rang like a fire alarm had gone off, and his vision tunneled.

"Holy shit!" Edwin shouted. He patted his chest and torso.

"Fuck," Jerry said.

"It missed you." Mia gestured with the gun. "Hit the window."

"You're crazy, lady!" Edwin's eyes were wild, face red. "By the time I get done with you, your whole family will be in prison."

Jerry grabbed her by the arm, but Mia resisted. She stood tall, focused completely on Edwin again. "What are you doing?"

"New plan. If the DA has no star witness, they'll drop the charges against Cody."

"Maybe," Jerry said.

"No. I know."

"You won't get away with this!" Edwin said.

A subtle smile found Mia's face. Her green eyes gleamed.

"I don't plan to," she said.

"Give me the gun, Mia," Jerry said.

"No."

Jerry repeated himself, emphasized each word. "Give. Me. The. Gun."

"Why?" She shot him a look.

"You were right. I'm the reason we're in this mess. I gave up on Cody. I didn't bail him out. I ran away from our problems. So, I should be the one to do this."

"What, and break the law?"

"I'd rather go to prison for something I did that was right than for Cody to go to prison for something he didn't even do."

"Touching family moment, really." Edwin cleared his throat. "Seriously, though. Put the gun down. I'll instruct my lawyer to withdraw my testimony. I swear."

Mia kept the gun aimed at Edwin. Then, motioned for Jerry to take it. They switched places, and she smoothly relinquished the gun to Jerry.

Once in his hands, it felt like it weighed a thousand pounds and nothing at the same time.

Jerry took a deep breath and moved his finger to the trigger.

THE TARANTULADOR

by Jim Ruland

The Poet

He blows on his coffee and contemplates the view from the second-story sitting room where he scratches out his poems. It's cool here in the morning, regardless of the season, but it's always colder outside. At this hour the only people out are the dog walkers. When the poet moved to the coast two years ago—or was it three?—there were dogs everywhere: lounging in the sun, roaming the beaches, begging for scraps in town. Now he seldom sees a stray unless he visits one of the neighboring villages.

Across the street sits the artist's compound, and beyond the trees he can see the ocean. The northern limit of the artist's property gives way to a densely timbered patch of land that drops away to form the southern slope of a steep canyon that tumbles into the cove below. On a wide, round berm, which the poet can see from his window, a trail winds down to the shore, but no one ever goes in the water in Punta de Tralca.

At sunset, locals and tourists gather at the overlook to watch "the show," as the poet likes to call it. He almost never goes because the view from the sitting room is fine. He can hear the crash of the surf, which is always intense, even with the windows closed, and watch the birds: grey gulls, stately pelicans, and lately, a condor of immense size that he sometimes catches a glimpse of as it circles the cove at the dark edge of dawn, like a great shadow that has torn loose from the night.

He doesn't like going to the overlook, because instead of watching the sun set, his eye is drawn to the tumult of the waves crashing on the boulders below. It is a violent place that spits up bits of broken boats on the shore all year long. The tourists come to watch the sun sink into the sea, but sometimes they fall in, and sometimes they die—and it's not always an accident.

The woman with the baby stroller is a grim reminder of this. She's been coming to the overlook every morning for the last three months, maybe more. The villagers have been gossiping about her for at least that long. They say she comes because her husband was swept away by the waves while taking a selfie, his back turned to the surf, which is something a local would never do. His phone was recovered but he was taken.

She comes with the baby, the man's infant son, in the hope that his body will wash up in the cove. Some people in the village say it wasn't an accident, that the man hurled himself off the cliff onto the rocks below and was sucked out to sea.

The poet doesn't care what the people in the village say. The people in the village are idiots. The poet knows they talk about him because they treat him like a tourist even though he's been living here for two or three years. The only person who talks to him like a local is Maria at the empanada shop, who always remembers his order—a double espresso and a cheese empanada—and never fails to ask about the book he brings with him to read while he waits.

"What's that you're reading?" she asks.

"Poetry," he says.

"Neruda?" Maria always asks.

"No, not Neruda," he replies with a smile.

It's a game they play. That's what the poet has decided. He hates Neruda. Has hated Neruda's poetry long before it became fashionable to hate the man. Neruda is long dead, but he had a house about a mile down the coast in Isla Negra. The house is still there. The poet supposes it's still Neruda's house because it's a museum now. Just once the poet would like Maria to guess "Parra," who lived a bit farther down the coast in Las Cruces and, as far as the poet knows, wasn't an asshole like Neruda.

Lately, Maria has been asking him about the widow and her baby, if she's still making her morning vigil on the overlook. He responds with a solemn nod, and the silence rushes in like the tide, seawater filling in the channels, forming pools that are cold and deep. He admires the widow's refusal to go back to the city until she learns her husband's fate.

The poet would like to do something for this woman. Writing a poem for her is out of the question. He would like to break the spell that compels her to come day after day, though he supposes he would miss her.

The poet wasn't always a poet. He used to be a musician. He used to write songs and sing them in front of small crowds of people. He would use a piano or a guitar, whatever was handy, to write them, though he didn't play an instrument on stage so he could focus on the words and their impact. He'd taken lessons in both instruments when he was a boy. He has a guitar but seldom plays it, only when he has something to say, something that can only be expressed in music, which is very much the situation now. Would a song lift the widow out of her sadness or deepen it?

The poet supposes it would depend on the song. He sips his coffee, but it has already gone cold.

The Widow

She doesn't know how much longer she can do this. When she first started coming here, she was certain she would find him, that he would come back to her.

When one of her many uncles was disappeared from Santiago in the early days of the dictatorship, the family received word that he had been taken to a makeshift detention center near the Mapocho River and executed. Every day, or so the story went, her grandmother would go to the bridge and wait for his body to wash downstream. There were plenty of bodies in the river in those days, but none of them that passed under her grandmother's watchful eye belonged to her son. It turned out he hadn't been murdered after all. He'd been put before a fake firing squad and given a mock execution, which was how the story of his death got started. After her uncle was released, he went to the coast to hide out for a few weeks without telling anyone. When he told the story at family gatherings, he always made it sound like a holiday that he spent holed up in a hotel drinking at the bar, while across the room her grandmother seethed in silence.

The story stayed with Tamara, and when Eugenio disappeared at the cove, she felt called to wait for him because she is convinced that whatever happened to her husband was no accident. Eugenio wasn't clumsy and he didn't kill himself. Eugenio loved her, and he loved their son, Andrés, but what he loved most of all was playing football with his friends every Saturday. He never missed a day. For Eugenio, it was more than a way to stay fit—he was in excellent shape—but he loved the camaraderie of those sessions, the competitiveness, the shit-talking. Those Saturdays were like therapy for him. Suicide? No chance. Not her Eugenio. So she will wait for him and prove to all those idiots in the village that what happened to her husband was unnatural. Do they think she doesn't notice what is going on in this terrible place?

Tamara isn't from here, but she's heard the talk. First the dogs started disappearing. Then it was the wild horses. They suddenly vanished as if an ark dropped out of the sky and they all climbed aboard and—whoosh!—off they went. The villagers assume the horses will be back, that they headed off in search of fresh grass. It has been a hot, dry summer. Tamara doesn't argue with that, but she knows that whatever did away with the dogs and spooked the horses has something to do with her husband's disappearance, has something to do with that thing she saw down in the cove.

In the deepest part of the ravine, there's something like a forest, a thick grove of bushes and trees that makes walking there impossible. In the center of that grove sits a shack. You can't see it from the cove, and from the overlook only the roof is visible. At first she thought it was abandoned, but then she noticed smoke coming from its chimney.

Tamara didn't think anything of it until Eugenio went missing and the police taped off the entrance to the cove and started asking her questions like "Was your husband depressed?" That's when she knew they weren't serious about finding Eugenio. What they were looking for was a reason *not* to look for him.

She showed them the last photo he'd taken on his phone—a selfie—and he was smiling, not a hint of melancholy. The rest of the photos were of the baby and his friends playing football.

"Does that look like someone who is suicidal?" she shouted.

"We're just trying to ascertain what his mood might have been at the time of the incident," said the detective.

"Was your husband a heavy drinker?" asked another.

"Why don't you ask the man who lives in the shack," she shouted. She was raving now and couldn't stop herself.

"No one has lived there for years," they said.

That was a lie. Tamara went to the overlook the following morning and every morning afterward. A few days ago, she saw someone on that little strip of sand between the rocks and the trees. It's too small to call a beach, though that's what it is. It was early in the morning and mostly dark. The baby had been crying all night, and she left the house earlier than usual because riding in the stroller calmed Andrés. She couldn't see very clearly, but from the overlook it appeared as if the figure was hunched over and wrapped in an old blanket. Maybe it's the person who lives in the shack, she thought. He might know something.

Tamara raced down the path, leaving Andrés in his stroller under the trees. She didn't give it a second thought. She just left him. She must have been out of her mind. She went a little crazy after what happened to Eugenio. She hasn't been eating or sleeping much. All she does is take care of the baby, and at the end of the day she remembers nothing. What they did, the food she ate, the programs that leaked out of the TV. Andrés, who senses that his father is missing, is inconsolable. He wails night and day. When she saw that figure on the beach, she took leave of her senses and ran. She somehow made it down the treacherous path without breaking her neck or twisting an ankle, and when she reached the bottom, she lost sight of the shack, that's how big the rocks are down there. From up above they look so small, but down there they are massive. It's louder too. The noise from the waves bounces around the boulders, and when they crash, you can feel it in your bones. It's overwhelming. She found the little beach and saw the figure in front of the shack. In the half-light of breaking dawn, she could see its greasy blanket, and as she approached, she detected a foul odor that told her this person lived down here in the shack, but as she drew closer, a switch flipped in her mind, telling her she was wrong, that this figure on the beach wasn't a man at all, but something else.

She stopped short. The thing on the beach rose up a few inches. Like a bird, she thought, and she saw that what she'd mistaken for a blanket was actually feathers on wings so gargantuan they could swallow a person and make him disappear. She had seen condors before, everyone has, but not up close, not like this. She was mistaken here, too, because although that thing on the beach had the body of a bird, when it turned its head, it regarded her with multiple sets of eyes, each black and unblinking like an insect's, arranged over a pair of long and hairy fangs.

Tamara screamed.

She screamed her lungs out, startling the creature so that it rose up with a great beating of wings and a blast of air that carried the sickening smell of death. She ran up the path and fled the overlook with her baby, promising herself that she would never leave Andrés alone again.

She resumed her vigil the next day, but she stays on the overlook, watching the beach. The man who lives in the yellow house down the street sits on the bench, playing his guitar. It's never a song she recognizes, but she likes it. He doesn't sing, for which she is grateful, but he often looks like he is thinking very deeply about something, as if he is going over the lyrics in his mind. It's the silence after he plays she likes best. That sounds cruel, but what she means is the pauses between the songs are intentional and feel like invitations. Here's a place where you could say something, the silence seems to say.

She hasn't spoken to the musician yet but likes knowing that she could, that it would not be unwelcome. Today she's going to ask him if he's ever seen anyone in the shack, and no matter what he says, she's going to tell him what she saw. She's going to wait until he stops playing; then she's going to break her silence and tell him what she saw down there in the cove.

The Scientist

It's not that serious, Sebastian thinks as he studies the mound of feathers at his feet. They are black and oily, the shafts sturdy and thick. Some of them are nearly as long as his arm. There are nearly twenty in all, and he adds them to the pile.

The specimen needs to eat. That much is plain. It's been huddled in the corner of the shack for days. Usually it tracks his movements around the place, especially when he enters and exits, but Sebastian hasn't gone anywhere in days, which is part of the problem. It needs to feed. The lack of nourishment is making it sluggish and slow, and now it's losing its feathers, which can't be good.

Sebastian can't believe it's come to this: hiding out in a fisherman's shack with no electricity or indoor plumbing. Six months ago he was promoted to lead researcher at the Institute. "Another promotion," his colleagues said, "and you'll be running this place."

Sebastian smiled and shook his head because that's not what he wanted. Sebastian loved the lab. Conducting experiments was what gave his life meaning. That didn't happen in meetings and on conference calls. The lab was where real science happened. Without regular access to the lab, he wouldn't be able to pursue his own experiments, experiments the Institute would never sanction. When the bureaucrats found out what Sebastian was up to, they fired him immediately. At least they did it quietly, without referring him to an ethics review, which would have crucified him. Nobody wanted that.

Luckily, Sebastian had already smuggled his experiment out of the lab. That's probably what got him caught: footage from a security camera of him leaving the Institute in the middle of the night with a specimen. He put the cage on a cart, covered it with a blanket, and rolled it out to his car. That's where he went wrong. "What's Sebastian hiding?" they must have wondered. Then they went to his lab and found out.

Yes, he took the specimen home. It was so small back then, but it had a voracious appetite. It was hungry all the time and needed to be fed. He couldn't risk keeping it at the Institute. The experiment was too...unusual. He took the specimen to the apartment he rented on the outskirts of the city and fed it mice he bought from the pet store, but it would only eat them if they were dead, which was disappointing, the first indication that his experiment had failed. It wasn't a total loss. The creature itself was stunning, a wonder to behold, but Sebastian hadn't sufficiently taken into account what the unintended consequences might be.

His specialty at the Institute was endangered species, identifying environmental factors that determined whether a particular species would thrive or die. Two of the animals that were most at risk in the Southern Cone were the Andean condor and the Goliath blood-drinker tarantula.

Consider the tarantula: one of the most feared species of arachnid. Despite its fearsome-looking fangs, the Goliath blood-drinker is neither venomous nor aggressive. It is simply a self-sufficient hunter. Andean condors, however, are grossly inefficient in that they are carrion eaters. They aren't predators. They eat the dead. Sebastian studied the problem and concluded that if he could make the condors a bit more efficient, or even aggressive, they could thrive in the rapidly shrinking habitats being encroached upon by development, deforestation, and mining operations that, in his opinion, were turning the country into an open sewer.

Sebastian tackled the problem in the lab and arrived at an innovative solution. The next step, he believed, was to get the specimen in the wild to see what it was capable of. That's when the experiment went downhill.

First, he lost his job, which wasn't the end of the world, but it was hardly ideal. He had enough savings to get by for a few months. He set up a makeshift laboratory in his apartment, which was practically in the foothills, and built a cage on the balcony. After withholding a few feedings, he set the specimen loose one night and watched it take flight toward the mountains, but instead of soaring into the skies, it returned almost immediately, clearly agitated. He repeated the experiment the next day at dusk and again the following morning at dawn. Each time, the specimen did a quick circle around the apartment complex and returned to Sebastian's balcony. He wanted to try again during the day but was afraid of what his neighbors would say. After those initial sorties, the specimen refused to even leave his balcony, and the creature cried out in hunger. The mice weren't cutting it anymore. It needed larger carcasses.

That night, Sebastian went out and found a dead dog on the side of the highway and brought it home for the specimen. He was relieved when it devoured the poor thing, but also a little disgusted. While the specimen feasted, Sebastian thought about the problem. That night he did some tests and confirmed his suspicions. The eyes of a tarantula were ideal for hunting in close, confined spaces, but they weren't the eyes of a condor. He'd inadvertently robbed the specimen of its most valuable weapon: its incredible vision.

As the specimen continued to grow, feeding it became a full-time job. Sebastian drove farther and longer in search of roadkill. Meanwhile, he passed live dogs by the dozens. These weren't pets but strays that were only nominally looked after. It was a simple thing to lure these flea-infested curs with meat laced with tranquilizers into his car. Then he transported the dogs back to his apartment. He killed them in the shower, cutting their throats with a cleaver with the shower running, while the specimen watched from the toilet tank with its multiple unblinking eyes, waiting to pounce on the dog after it took its last breath. There were complaints from the neighbors about the smell, yes, but Sebastian got used to it. A lifetime in the lab had acclimated him to all kinds of horrors, but the noise the specimen made was a problem, especially when it was hungry, which was always.

It must be said that feeding the specimen brought him closer to it, and it to him. The condor with the face of a tarantula was fond of rubbing its hairy forelegs on Sebastian's hands in a way that could only be described as affectionate. By withholding food or altering its feeding schedule, Sebastian was able to teach it all kinds of things, and he grew to appreciate the specimen's extraordinary intelligence. It was responsive to touch and seemed to enjoy being groomed, but would only allow Sebastian to clean its forelegs and wipe down its fangs after a feeding.

Still the specimen grew, and after a neighbor reported strange sounds she heard coming from Sebastian's balcony, the property manager insisted on inspecting the unit. That, he could not allow. The apartment had strict policies about pets, and he was certain it wouldn't make an exception for his specimen.

It was time to go.

Instead of driving into the mountains, the condor's natural habitat, Sebastian drove to the coast where his cousin had a small ranch. When he was a child, he would spend holidays there with his family, grilling fish they caught themselves. Sebastian knew that his cousin had a girlfriend in Santiago and was seldom at the ranch. He would go to the coast for a few weeks while he figured out what to do. He needed to teach the specimen how to survive in the wild, and he couldn't do that in his apartment.

When he reached the coast, he was in for a shock: His cousin's ranch, which had provided so many fond memories when he was a child, had been sold. The ranch was now a daycare center, and his cousin was nowhere to be found. Sebastian was disconsolate. Driving to the beach, he remembered the shack at the bottom of the cove where they used to clean their catch before taking it home. The shack was still there, but it was abandoned and in disrepair. This was where he would conduct his final experiments with the specimen.

Sebastian got a small fire going, and after setting up a makeshift lab, he went looking for feed. He didn't like killing dogs. Dogs never gave him any trouble. People were the problem. Destroying habitats, ruining ecosystems, making the planet uninhabitable for so many innocent creatures, driving them to extinction. It hardly seemed fair, to him and to the dogs, while the rich burned up the atmosphere with their private jets, luxury yachts, fleets of automobiles. All these people did was take. He had given the world a majestic new species for which they would call *him* a monster.

His money gone, he lived on small fish he smoked in the shack. He tried to maintain a feeding schedule, but he couldn't keep up. He was running out of dogs. The specimen was always hungry, and its cries were like nothing he'd ever heard. It was so awful, so pathetic, that anyone with an ounce of compassion would do anything to make it stop. He tried to lure one of the wild horses to the cove but spooked the entire herd. The specimen's cries kept him awake at night, and when he could sleep, the pounding of the waves invaded his dreams. He was trapped in a nightmare from which he couldn't wake. Sebastian started to question his sanity.

The first person he killed was a man who knocked on the shack's door, asking if he'd seen his dog. The man was a tourist, passing through town on his way down the coast. He'd stopped to let his dog get some exercise, and he swore he saw it run down the path to the cove. The man was so frantic that he passed his mania on to Sebastian, who in fact hadn't seen his dog, though it would turn up later, and he brained the man with an iron bar. The man collapsed, and Sebastian dragged him inside the shack. The specimen was excited by the kill but seemed to hesitate, as if waiting for Sebastian's approval. He removed the man's wallet and keys and said what he always said when presenting the creature with its feed:

"Go ahead, my sweet."

The specimen fed on the man's carcass for hours, and then, when the dog showed up and Sebastian killed it, the specimen devoured that, too.

The second person was an older man Sebastian found reading a book. The third was a fool who went way out on the rocks, tempting fate for a photograph. Sebastian would do whatever it took to protect the specimen. Despite being just steps from the sea, an air of death clung to the shack.

Even though he failed to cultivate a more aggressive specimen, it continued to grow into something magnificent, a marvel of science and nature. Sebastian dreamed of showing it to his former colleagues at the Institute so that they could gawk in wonder at the beauty that he had created. He fantasized about the accolades he would receive, a fully funded laboratory with his name on it at the most illustrious university in the Americas—if only his colleagues had his courage, his *vision*. These dreams were disrupted by the casual cruelty that caring for the specimen required.

The creature is now bigger than him and can no longer fit in his car—or any car for that matter. If the specimen spreads its wings inside the shack, it can touch the walls at both ends of the flimsy structure. It is too risky to let the specimen fly during the day—it would attract too much attention. Sebastian tried to train the creature at night. Despite its gargantuan size, instead of being emboldened by the outdoors, the specimen grew more timid. He tried locking it out of the shack, but instead of taking flight, it huddled on the rocks until the tide came in and the sun came up and Sebastian let it back inside.

The specimen is helpless without him. Instead of soaring in the sky, it possesses the arachnid's instinct to burrow. It has turned the shack into a warren of rags and bones. While the specimen's size and appetite grows, Sebastian's hope for his experiment shrinks. He wonders if he is poisoning himself with fumes from the fire or mercury from the fish because he is tired all the time and cannot sleep. His thoughts are disordered, and his days of scientific study feel distant and remote. His hours are organized by a creature that cares not if he lives or dies but demands to be fed. He is always hunting for driftwood and fish for himself, and meat for his master, for that's what the specimen has become—a great god—and he is its faithful servant.

During feeding time, Sebastian listens to the specimen strip the flesh and silver the bones, and he knows that he isn't long for this world. When it is hungry, the creature watches over Sebastian with unusual intensity. He imagines the specimen spreading its wings over him and devouring him piece by piece, its multiple eyes studying him like a butcher with a calf he'd raised for slaughter. This is his destiny, Sebastian realizes, to become one with his creation.

That day is coming, but it isn't here yet. Sebastian has his eye on the young woman and her baby who come to the overlook each day as if offering themselves as a sacrifice for the terrible god they can feel stirring below. She came down to the cove while he was out foraging and left her child unsupervised. He could have scooped up the baby in his arms, but they were full of firewood.

If only he could lure her back to the shack, he would not squander such an opportunity again.

The Empanada Maker

Maria eyes the skinny little journalist with suspicion. She'd been in the shop earlier that morning and had ordered a coffee, no milk, and a vegetable empanada, which only the rich tourists from the city bought and never more than once, because without meat, cheese, or lard, they tasted terrible, but that's what they thought they wanted.

Now the journalist is back, and although the customers have cleared out, Maria still has plenty to do: special orders to prepare, supplies to inventory, deliveries to arrange. Her work is never done. When the woman starts asking questions about the cove, Maria knows exactly why she's here.

"You want to know about the cannibal? You're a little late, aren't you?"

When the story broke, journalists from all over the country descended on the village. Everyone wanted to know about the mad scientist who ate dogs and people and made an altar out of their bones in an abandoned shack down in the cove full of feathers and fur. Horrible stuff but it had been good for the village and especially Maria's empanada shop, which has the best empanadas on the coast, anyone will tell you that, but weeks have passed since the cannibal tried to snatch a baby from a stroller on the overlook and a musician, one of her regular customers who had taken to keeping the mother company, beat the cannibal with his guitar and threw him off the cliff.

"I just have a few questions," the woman asks.

"I've told all there is to tell," Maria insists. If someone from the village had been involved, then it would be a different story. Maria could tell the journalist their whole history. But they were all tourists. Even the dead ones. Tourists come and tourists go. That may sound harsh, but that's the way it is in this part of the world.

"Didn't the musician live here?" the journalist asks.

Maria scowls. She thinks of him often. He is the part of the story that belongs to her. "Two years, maybe three, but for those of us who were born here and will die here, that is no more than a long weekend. People lay claim to the coast all the time, like that famous poet."

"Neruda?"

"Yes, but he is not one of us. Put that in your newspaper."

The journalist shifts, sets her jaw, and it is like Maria can read her mind: *This woman with her shitty empanadas is giving me attitude.* Maybe Maria is mistaken because the woman smiles and says she isn't a journalist. She's from a research institute dedicated to helping endangered species.

"Ah," Maria says. "You've heard about the tarantulador."

Maria has a cousin whose husband is a dispatcher at the police station, and when the police went to sort out the mess—the cannibal's brains all over the cliff, the horrors inside the shack— the widow whose husband had disappeared and whose baby had almost been snatched raved like a madwoman about a creature that was half condor, half tarantula.

"Yes," the woman from the Institute says. "I know."

Maria decides to give her a bone, so to speak. "A funny thing happened," she says. "When the widow made her formal statement to the police, she didn't mention anything about a creature. She said she was deranged from lack of sleep."

"Do you believe her?" the woman from the Institute asks.

"About the creature?"

The woman nods.

"I believe that poor woman is gone. I believe she left with the musician, who was also a poet, did you know that? I believe they will make more babies and they won't be coming back. Why would they?"

"And the…tarantulador?" the journalist asks. "Have you seen it?"

Maria shakes her head. "I believe there is a creature that flies over the cove at night, a creature that flies so high that you can't hear its wings beating, a creature so big that you can see its silhouette when the moon is full and its shadow crawls across the cove. I believe it is hunting for something, and when it finds it, it will disappear."

"That's it?"

Maria pauses to consider this skinny little woman from the Institute.

"I believe when you are hungry, you should listen to what your body desires."

WOUNDED THINGS

by C.W. Blackwell

Joe Beltran's old knees clicked one after the other as he swung his legs over the bow of the *Delia Blue*. Night fog lay thick on the harbor, sunrise still an hour off. The tide was out, and the boat sat low in its moorings, rafts of dead sardines bobbing whitely against black water like discarded cigarettes. His deckhand, Virge, had done a half-ass job cleaning after the last booking, and he couldn't tell how much reek came from the sardines in the harbor or from the fish guts clotted over everything in sight.

He slipped his cell phone from the inside of his fleece jacket and mashed his thumb onto Virge's contact. The call went straight to voicemail.

"This is a wake-up call," said Beltran. "Goddammit, wake up and call me."

He'd paid Virge two days ago, and he had a suspicion his deckhand was doing what he did best—blowing his paycheck on late nights at the downtown bars with his cheap girlfriends and baseball buddies. Maybe he hadn't even made it to bed by now. Beltran decided that this would be it. If Virge didn't show for this morning's booking, then he wouldn't have use for him again.

The party arrived at six thirty—a trio of tech workers dressed oddly in heavy winter jackets, cocaine rimming their steaming nostrils. They commented how the *Delia Blue* was shockingly small and the photos on the website were misleading. The alpha of the group was a thin man with hair plugs and Botoxed eyes named Barry Gartz. He stood with his arms folded, looking over the boat as if reconsidering the whole trip.

"I don't know, boys," he said, rolling his lips to the side. "It's definitely not Holstrom's yacht, am I right?"

"Where's the stabbin' cabin?" joked his friend, and they all laughed.

"Well, she ain't the newest boat in the harbor," said Beltran, summoning the charm he'd cultivated to lure fat-walleted tourists for the past twenty years, "but she's the fastest. That means we'll be yanking vermilion out of the bay twenty minutes before anyone else. You'll be the talk of the office come Monday, believe me."

"Can you knock a few bucks off for the deceptive ad?"

"You already paid, my friend."

"Sure, but you can reverse the charge and give us a discount, right?"

Beltran hid his disdain well.

"Let's talk about it after you fill your coolers, boys. Hear those gulls calling out? The sun's about to rise."

* * *

Virge never showed.

Beltran worked the whole booking himself—the sonar, the

navigation, baiting the hooks. They'd forgotten a bottle opener, so he even had to crack open their West Coast IPAs as they stood drinking and tugging their lines, bantering about the time they took Holstrom's yacht under the Golden Gate Bridge and up the coast with three blond escorts from Nevada. They must have used the word *epic* to describe their bourgeois adventures more times than he'd heard in his life up until now.

They caught their limit by noon, and soon after, Beltran was motoring back to the harbor with his drunken passengers. One had even stood atop the stern and pissed off the back of the boat, but Beltran didn't say a word. He didn't want to give them a reason to haggle down the price or trash his business online. Instead, he flattered their fishing skills and had them pose with their mediocre catches.

"This is going to make the website," he said, convincingly enough. "Best catch of the season, by far."

Later, as Beltran sprayed the deck and flung the stringy guts into the water for the gulls and crabs, he found Barry Gartz's eel-skin wallet wedged into a seat cushion like a shiny gray book. People had left things before—wallets, purses, fanny packs—but what was different was the nearly two thousand dollars in cash, the small baggie of cocaine, and the one-ounce palladium coin slotted deep into one of the wallet's compartments. He took the coin out and turned it over. He would have thought it was silver had he not studied the letters curving around the beveled edge. He'd have to look up exactly what palladium was and how much it was worth when he got home, but he wagered it was worth more than a cooler full of rockfish.

"Shit," he said to himself. "That's a hell of a tip, Barry."

He went into the dark of the cabin and flipped through the party's contact information and dialed Gartz's number. No answer. He dialed again and left a message, telling him he'd found the wallet and to call back, but by the time the boat was clean and the gear had been put away, Gartz still hadn't returned his call. Beltran zipped out of his reeking jumpsuit, shoved the wallet into the front pocket of his jeans, and hiked out to his rust bucket F-150 and headed for home.

* * *

It was still light out when he pulled off the redwood highway toward his leaf-smothered, two-bedroom cabin. When he entered through the side door, he found Oliver sitting at the kitchen table with his laptop open and a few sheets of paper marked up in pencil. It took Beltran a moment to figure out what was different about the boy, but when he saw the thrift-store wheelchair sitting empty in the hallway, he smiled and laid the day's mail on the kitchen counter, giving each bill a mindless glance.

"Did you walk from the hall to the kitchen?"

"Yep," said Oliver without looking up. The pencil made a hissing sound as he circled some algebraic solution. "Six steps from there to here."

"That's great, kiddo. But do you think it was a good idea to do it alone?"

"I wasn't alone. Uncle Virge was here."

"Oh?"

"He made breakfast and watched me in case I fell, but I didn't fall."

Beltran opened the refrigerator and noted the single egg remaining in the carton and two Budweisers missing from the six-pack carrier. He was still upset with Virge for making his day harder than it had needed to be, but at least he'd done something useful for the boy. He took a pound of ground chuck from the bottom shelf, inspected the expiration date, and set it on the counter.

"So the leg pain's not so bad today?" asked Beltran. He pretended he was only half interested whenever he asked about the pain. He didn't want to make it the biggest thing in the boy's life, even though it's all Beltran worried about. He also knew that Oliver's pain made him think of his mom and dad, and that opened up a whole catalog of emotions that wouldn't be sorted for a while, if ever. "Don't forget you have PT tomorrow afternoon. It's with that new therapist with the nose ring."

The pencil stopped scratching for a moment.

"Grandpa?"

"What, kiddo?"

"I want to go back to school. In person, not remote."

Beltran mixed the ground beef by hand with salt and pepper and added a splash of milk to make the patties juicier and more tender. It was something he'd taught his daughter, and it was what Oliver was used to. He squared the buns face down on the griddle and set it to low so they'd toast while the burgers cooked, and he dotted the patties with tiny slivers of butter.

"Did you hear me?" said Oliver.

"Yeah, kiddo. I just don't know who'd take you back and forth, is all. My schedule is all over the place."

"Maybe Uncle Virge could do it?"

"Virge can't even make it to work on time," he said with a dismissive laugh—and the way he said it almost sounded cruel. "That would be one heartache after another, let me tell you. There's people in this world you can count on and people you can't. Every family's got their own mix."

"He showed up for breakfast."

"On his own time, sure. Everything is on his own time with that one."

"I forgot to tell you—there's a bus stop on Bear Creek Road." Oliver sounded like he'd had an epiphany. "I could get there without anyone's help if I had an electric scooter. I've seen other kids riding them."

"How much do those cost?"

Oliver clicked at the laptop.

"Here's a used one with a seat—five hundred dollars. That's not a lot of money, is it?"

"It's not a little, either." Beltran placed the hamburger patties on a baking pan and fired up the broiler. He pictured Barry Gartz and his tech buddies cruising up the coast eating Wagyu beef sliders while topless blondes shuffled around with vapid thousand-dollar-a-day smiles. They could keep their fancy meats and plastic tits—Beltran took satisfaction knowing that he stood where he was most needed. "Why don't we ask your therapist about it tomorrow? It'll be good to get an expert opinion."

"Riding a scooter is easy," said Oliver, bristling. "Is it the money?"

"It's not about the money. Let's just ask first, okay?"

* * *

Next morning, Beltran called Gartz's number from the back porch of the cabin. As he rattled off another message in the cool of the redwoods with a steaming cup of coffee in his hand, he felt a growing unease, and he couldn't tell if it arose from the cocaine in the billfold, the thick wad of hundred-dollar bills, or the notion that Gartz was in some kind of trouble. He thought about turning the wallet over to the police, but he knew the drugs might cause a problem for Gartz—and avoiding a problem like that might be worth some kind of reward. He set down the coffee and flipped through the wallet again. Credit cards, a security key. He remembered when folks would keep family photos tucked into brittle plastic holders inside their wallets—maybe a wedding photo, a baby picture. Cherished images. He remembered how they would fade and peel and become burned-looking over time, but to him, it was somehow better than having every photo you've ever taken on an endless digital scroll in your pocket.

His phone rang—it was Virge.

"Hey, I'm here at the harbor," said Virge. "Where is everyone?"

"You're a whole day late. No bookings today."

"I swore you told me Sunday."

"I did. It's Monday, dummy." Beltran let the last part slip—he'd promised not to call him that anymore. "Why don't you give the boat a deep clean, and I'll consider keeping you on the books for another week. The cabin, the head, everything. We got a triple-booking this weekend, so make it sparkle."

"Aye, aye, Captain. Did you use the new digital liability waiver I made?"

"Yeah, it worked fine. Saved a little time, I guess."

"That's good. How's O-Dog?"

"He's all right. He wants an electric scooter."

"How much are those?"

"He says five hundred."

Virge whistled. "Kids are expensive, aren't they?"

Beltran didn't answer. Oliver's mother and father had left some money behind, but after the surgeries and endless physical therapy sessions, there wasn't much left. He'd also forgotten how much food teenagers consumed on a weekly basis. There would be more money from the Social Security office at some point, but they'd cut so much staffing that the paperwork kept getting held up.

"I'm headed to the Westside," said Beltran. "A client dropped their wallet in the boat and isn't returning my calls, so now I gotta hunt them down."

"A wallet? Any money in it?"

"Quite a bit, among other things."

"Sounds like scooter money to me."

"I'm trying to correct my karma, Virge. Clean the boat. I'll fill you in later."

* * *

He drove across town as the fog made a slow retreat into the bay. It was so thick it drenched the windshield like rain. When he came down Pacific Avenue with the windshield wipers groaning and screeching, he smelled the fresh beans and rice at the taqueria across from the Municipal Wharf. He'd skipped breakfast, and his stomach felt hollow. Gartz's house wasn't far, according to the address on the ID—he decided he'd get a fried taco on the way back, and a breakfast burrito for the boy.

The house was a two-story Tuscan-style villa with a terracotta roof and wrought iron bars composed along the balustrades. The yard looked well manicured. Jacarandas blooming along the stuccoed walls. Beltran parked along the street and double-checked the address and squinted at the teal mosaic street number to make sure he was in the right place. He assumed Gartz was wealthy, but not this wealthy. After a moment, he wandered up the brick walkway and knocked on the door using the iron knocker. The clang was louder than he expected, even though the fog dampened the sound. He waited. Music played in some far-off place, but he couldn't tell where it came from. There was also a constant grinding sound from somewhere on the upper floor.

He knocked again—nothing.

Built into the door was an aluminum mail slot. He hinged the slat open and peered inside. No movement. Just a dark parlor with expensive-looking furniture. A car passed slowly on the street, and he suddenly felt like a prowler.

Screw it, he thought. *I've done enough here.*

He slipped Gartz's wallet through the mail slot and heard it thump heavily onto the tile floor like a dog turd. Maybe there wouldn't be a reward, but at least he'd gotten rid of the damned thing.

Stepping off the front porch, he heard a woman's voice drifting from the side yard. Now a laugh—sort of a sarcastic tone. He realized the music was also coming from that direction. He crossed the front lawn to the gate and called out. The music continued, but the voice fell silent. He tugged at the gate and it creaked open. He called again. Looking down the side yard toward the back of the house, he could see an uncovered pool with someone leisurely floating there. He moved closer. It was a man with dark hair and a bald spot—maybe Gartz—but he was floating face down in the water in his pajamas, listing stiffly like a log after a storm. Beltran lunged for the edge of the pool to pull the man from the water—an instinct from decades on the sea.

"Don't bother," said a voice. "He's been floating there all morning."

Beltran looked up wildly, searching for the source of the voice.

A young woman stood on the threshold of the back door. Blond hair tied up into a wild mess, jean shorts so small they reached the crease of her thighs. She wore a plain men's T-shirt that she'd drawn into a knot at the waist, and Beltran could see there were spots where she'd bled through it—or perhaps she'd been bled upon.

"You the gardener or something?" she asked.

"No, not the gardener—have you called the police?" He was kneeling over the edge of the pool, trying to reach the body. Her hesitation gave him a chilling sensation. The blood, the lack of urgency. It wasn't how anyone would behave in this situation. "Have you?"

"We sort of got it taken care of," she said, leaning into the jamb, crossing her feet at the ankles. "You should probably just leave."

"Who's we?" Beltran kicked off his boots and set his phone, keys, and wallet on the lip of the pool and jumped into the water, pushing off toward the center. When he reached the body, it felt cold and rigid. He could just touch the bottom with the pads of his feet, so he towed the body into shallow water and tipped it so he could see the face. Heavy, swollen cheeks. Graying eyes. But he recognized him as Barry Gartz. "I don't know what you think you've 'taken care of,'" said Beltran, "but you need to call the police and have the coroner take this body in."

"You're making it worse for yourself," said the woman.

Beltran raised his voice. "Worse, how?"

Another figure appeared behind her—a tall man with a trucker hat and an unkempt goatee that clung to his face like bad taxidermy. He edged past the woman and stood looking over the scene with a pistol in one hand and nylon rope in the other. He clicked his teeth and shook his head sadly, as if judging a bad piece of art.

"I'm gonna need you to get on out of the pool," said the man.

"Who the fuck are you?"

The man dropped the rope on the ground and scratched at the coarse whiskers on his jaw with the barrel of the gun.

"I don't like repeating myself, Mr. Old Man. Just do what I say, all right?"

* * *

The woman held the gun on him while the man tied his wrists and ankles. From their bantering and bickering, he learned the woman's name was Ashley and the man went by Junior, who was doing some work upstairs, the sound of an industrial drill shrieking through a slab of metal. Junior came down in fifteen-minute intervals, and Ashley would ask him if he was close, and he would stand there flipping a large coin—maybe another palladium coin from Gartz's stash. He studied Beltran as if deciding what must be done with him.

"I have to be somewhere soon," said Beltran. "People are depending on me."

"One thing at a time, old man," said Junior. There were burn marks on his sweatshirt from sparks that had cast off during his upstairs labor. A safe, perhaps. Or a vault. "Unless you're good with power tools. Then maybe we can reach some kind of mutually beneficial agreement."

"I don't want to help you. But I wouldn't say shit if you untied me and let me go."

"If you kept quiet, that would still be helping us, wouldn't it?" He directed the question at Ashley as if she were some kind of referee, and she bobbed her head in agreement. "Maybe it's neither here nor there, but that man Gartz weren't no saint, if you know what I mean. The world won't miss him. Show him, Ash."

"I don't wanna show him nothing," she said. She was fixing herself a drink at the wet bar, chasing ice cubes around a highball glass. "What the hell does it matter, anyway?"

Junior insisted. "It's relevant information, baby. Just show him."

Ashley rolled her lazy, drunken eyes. She set the highball down and untied the knot in her T-shirt and lifted it all the way up past her collarbones. Beltran glanced at the bloody crescent shapes there.

"Ashley's a first-rate escort," said Junior. "She was up to two grand a night. You count all them bite marks, and we're dealing with immeasurable harm to her livelihood. We told Mr. Gartz not to do it again, and, well—" He gestured outside where the corpse was making a slow, stiff circle in the water. "He gone and done it again."

"So you two killed him?"

"You ever have your titties bit this hard?" said Ashley, pressing at the wounds tenderly.

"Can't say I've had them bit any which way," said Beltran.

"Well if you had, you'd know it's enough to want to kill a motherfucker."

"Listen, I'm raising my grandson," said Beltran. "That's one thing you need to know about me. My daughter and her husband died in a bus crash. My grandson was with them, and he nearly died himself. So I've seen more scars than you can count, okay? But I didn't kill anyone over it, and I'm not gonna make it worse by skipping out on my grandson's PT appointment today." He strained against the nylon rope and wriggled his fingers. "For the last goddamn time, just let me get on my way."

"How'd you know him, anyway?" asked Junior.

"Who?"

"Who do you think? Gartz. The titty biter."

"I run fishing tours out of the harbor. He was a customer."

"Fishing tours? You own a boat?"

"Don't get any ideas."

Junior and Ashley shared an enlightened glance.

* * *

Despite Beltran's refusals, the pair worked him into their escape plan. Once Junior finished drilling what he described as the "biggest safe I'd ever seen," he and Ashley would drive Beltran to the harbor in the trunk of their car and set a course for Santa Monica, where they planned to start their own adult entertainment company. No bus tickets to track, or rental car receipts or license plate readers—just the wide-open ocean and a southerly course.

When the garden clock on the wall read one p.m., Beltran couldn't take it anymore. He could hear his phone ding-ding-dinging. It sent him into a tirade of curse words and threats to retract his promise and turn them over to the police at his first opportunity.

"But you're not going to do that, are you?" said Junior from the stairwell.

"Like hell I'm not. It's the first goddamn thing I'll do once I get rid of you fuckers."

Junior turned to Ashley, who, by Beltran's count, was sucking on her fourth cocktail.

"Get his wallet," he told her.

"I'm not touching that old man," she said, tightening up her drink with a splash of vodka. She'd laid the pistol on the bar cart so she could work the fancy bar accoutrements. The coiled strainer. The muddler and the barspoon. "You want it so bad, you get it."

"It's laying right there by the edge of the pool, baby."

She rolled her eyes and slowly shuffled out the back door and swiped the wallet off the blue tile lip of the swimming pool. She didn't pause to consider the dead man, who'd drifted toward the deep end, where a trio of flies could be seen landing and launching from the soft hairs of his Rogained head. When she returned, she handed the wallet to Junior but let it fall to the ground before he could reach it.

"I don't work for you anymore," she said. She gave a malevolent look and resumed her activities at the wet bar. "So stop bossing me around."

Junior flipped through Beltran's wallet and wiggled out the driver's license he found there and recited the name and address three times as if he were announcing the winner of a monthly drawing.

"You said your grandson is living with you?"

"Fuck you," said Beltran.

"You said he doesn't get around so well, huh?"

He spit on the ceramic tile floor. "Fuck you twice."

"Tell you what, old man. You stop threatening us, and we won't threaten you. Or your grandson. Sounds like a fair deal, right?"

Beltran imagined Oliver waiting at the top of the porch ramp he'd built for him as the minutes ticked by. How long would the boy wait before turning back? It would be the first time Beltran let him down. He'd made mistakes, sure. It had been years since he'd parented a child, and some things had to be relearned. But he'd never left the boy stranded—not once. He decided if he were to try and make a play, if he were to get free somehow, it would have to be here at Gartz's house, with his truck parked nearby. Better than halfway down the coast on the *Delia Blue* with nothing but fog and kelp for miles around.

Beltran waited another thirty minutes while Junior rummaged through the refrigerator and cupboards looking for something to eat. He seemed oddly relaxed, given the soggy corpse in the pool and all the likely appointments the dead man was missing. When Junior finally went upstairs to finish his work, Beltran got Ashley's attention with a whistle.

"I have some cocaine if you want it," he said.

She gave a wild laugh, but her face settled into a curious stare.

"You want to party right now?"

"Not me. I was offering it to you."

"Where is it? In your old-man undies?" She said it jokingly, but her attention stayed put. "You aren't serious, are you?"

"It's why I'm here," said Beltran, nodding at the front door. "You probably couldn't hear it over the drilling, but I slipped

Gartz's wallet through the mail slot. He left it in my boat with a bunch of cash and a baggie of cocaine. At least I think it's cocaine."

She looked toward the door.

There it was.

She set down her drink—now a sick mauve concoction of all the exotic mixers she'd added—and padded barefoot across the parlor toward the front door. She glanced at Beltran as if it might be a trick, but curiosity finally got the better of her, and she squatted over the wallet and spread it open.

He watched her: drunk and distracted, thirty feet away, unarmed.

Beltran rose to his feet and shuffled out the back door.

* * *

With his ankles tied together, it took him an eternity to reach the edge of the pool, where he lowered himself over his car keys and phone. Another text notification from Oliver appeared on his phone, but he left it where it lay and kept inching toward the side gate with his keys clasped tightly in his bound hands. He'd made it about halfway along the length of the pool when Ashley came bolting into the backyard with the eel-skin wallet in one hand and the pistol in the other.

Beltran shuffled faster, but he was still only shuffling.

She took him by the shoulder and spun him with the pistol jammed under his chin, the reek of tropical fruit juice and vodka welling up around her. Cocaine clung to the tiny hairs of her nostrils.

"I don't see why Junior wants to keep you around so bad," she said, talking fast. "We'll be rich when he gets that safe open. It would be so much better to hire a driver to Santa Monica. Maybe a fancy car—a *Maserati*. Bet you never driven one of those, old man. I hate boats, anyway. God, I hate boats. They make me puke."

She kneed him hard in the thigh, and he buckled, lost his balance, and toppled backward into the pool. He managed a loud *help* before he hit the water. Then he began frantically working his bound wrists together as he dipped below the surface. Maybe the keys would give enough bite to cut through—maybe it would take far too long. Above, he could see her standing there, her warped blond figure watching him drown. In those moments before death, all he thought of was Oliver, and how sorry he was that he'd skipped out on him. Soon the boy would learn what had happened, and he would forgive him. But what trauma, then? What life would there be for a boy so touched by death?

He kept working his wrists together, but the knot was just too tight.

He looked up helplessly from the depths.

Ashley was still there, but now another figure appeared behind her. It wasn't Junior. She spun and raised the gun, and now he thought he saw the swing of a baseball bat. A dull crack. The water churned as she folded into the pool. He saw blood, a wreath of blond hair. Hard plastic tits bearing down on him like owl's eyes. Just as his consciousness began to fray, he felt himself rising to the surface.

Air rushed into his lungs.

Virge.

"Come on, old man," he said. "Let's get you untied."

Beltran coughed and heaved as Virge helped him up the painted steps and out of the pool. Ashley floated next to Barry Gartz in an inky cloud of blood. Together they looked like a pair of grim snorkelers drifting on a chummed sea.

"How'd you find me?" managed Beltran.

"You told me about the wallet, remember? I checked the liability waivers when you didn't show for Oliver's therapy session, and found the address. Man, who was that chick?"

The drilling on the second floor abruptly stopped, and both men looked up.

"There's a man up there," said Beltran. "I think it's her pimp."

"Her pimp?"

"Just get me the hell out of here, buddy."

They went dripping and stumbling toward the side gate, past the bloody baseball bat on the wet cement. Beltran spotted Gartz's wallet lying there—the eel-skin monstrosity that started the whole shit show. He stopped and knelt over it, slipped five hundred dollars from the billfold, and went on through the gate and across the front lawn where Virge's pickup sat idling at the curb.

* * *

Oliver was doing donuts on his new electric scooter when the police cruiser trundled up the dirt road. The scooter had a fair amount of torque, and the boy even managed to get Beltran to drive the thing down the driveway and back, kicking up a fine beige dust as he went. When the police detectives stepped from their car with their wrinkle-free shirts, matching ties, and belt badges, Beltran greeted them both with a cautious wave.

"That boy can really get around," said one of the cops—a midthirties man with a closely groomed beard. The fog had burned off early, and he stood shielding his eyes from the sun. "Maybe we'll race him back to town."

"You've got more horsepower, but he'll beat you on sheer determination."

The cop allowed this with a flip of his hands.

"Thought you'd want to know that Junior Barnes died in a firefight this morning with the Salinas PD. Caught up to him in the parking lot of an AMPM on the 101."

Beltran nodded as if he'd expected this. "Sounds like he barely made it out of the county."

"People don't get away with much these days. At least not things like that."

"And the woman?" Beltran glanced at Virge when he said it, who was putting out a cigarette on the sole of his boot. "She alive?"

"In the hospital. Brain damage, they say."

The other cop chimed in, gesturing at Virge, "We'll need another statement from your son-in-law. Just a formality. The DA doesn't want to pursue charges on him. But if they pull the plug on the escort, we'll need to have all the details in order."

"He's more of a nephew-in-law," said Beltran, but he promptly regretted putting so much genealogical distance between them. Virge had saved Beltran's life and prevented the boy from becoming a ward of the state. He'd earned a place in the family—whatever was left of it. "He didn't want to kill nobody. She was armed and I'll attest to it."

"And you didn't take anything from the property? We need to get that part right."

"No sir," said Beltran as Oliver made another gleeful lap around the driveway. He hadn't heard him laugh like that since last year, when the bottom dropped out of everything. Oliver howled and giggled like a kid half his age. It reminded Beltran of his own daughter a couple decades back, when the world made sense and wasn't yet such a dark and wounded thing. "I returned the man's wallet, that's all. Only thing I made off with is a little chlorine in my lungs, a bruised leg, and a ruined afternoon."

But as Oliver wheeled through the driveway—Virge egging him on with the comic solemnity of a bullfighter—Beltran wondered if it was only the past that was wounded now, and that most everything else had begun to heal. Maybe it happened quicker than he'd thought, that all you had to do was stop every now and then and count the scars.

Beltran called out to Oliver. "Take a break and come get yourself a glass of water," he said. "Give your old grandpa another turn on that thing."

THE COACHELLA DEATH PIXIE

by Nik Xandir Wolf

The tent was dark and quiet inside. A girl sat alone with headphones on, behind a makeshift desk of stacked crates and splintered planks. The air was heavy with smoke and dust and the slightly foul scent of stale body sweat.

"I was told that you are the person to see," I said, my chest tightening, hands slick, the room constricting inward. "If someone were to need a substance"—I lowered my voice to a whisper—"let's say, less than recreational and entirely undetectable."

The dreamy smile on her wan, cherublike face disappeared. She eyed me, eyebrows raised, lips tight. Her vibe was whimsical, mythical; a pixie, elf, or some sort of festival-generated hybrid. This was the spot. The pop-up pharmacist that the girl I'd hooked up with a few hours before had told me about. Everybody was on something, and this tent ostensibly dealt in typical festival drugs: Ecstasy, psilocybin, lysergic, MDMA. "The usual suspects and a little more," the girl had said, "something to help you with your problem partner." Based on this pixie's glower, I second-guessed my approach. A little more tact might have been exercised. But then again, how does one approach an underground pharmacist dispensing lethal doses of undetectable poison?

The silence between us grew unbearable, my heart sprinting in my chest like I'd just run a marathon. The thumping bass line from Doja Cat a football field away rattled in my chest, my heart skipped a beat, blood rushed in my ears. I wiped my palms dry on my shorts and breathed deeply to clear the weed-induced cobwebs from my rattled brain. Was I being paranoid, or was it that this tiny girl terrified me? Her sunken, birdlike, green eyes bored into my soul. Then, finally, she spoke.

"I do not know you. To trust you, we must drink tea together," she said. "And you must answer my questions."

I nodded. She stood and lashed the flaps to the tent closed, then walked toward the back, motioning me to follow, which I did. I hadn't known what to expect when I'd followed the advice of a twentysomething burner chick after we'd made sweaty, violent love to each other in my tent earlier today. But now, today, this was my only chance. So I'd forced my way through the percussively writhing mass of sweat-slick bodies to the edge of the music festival, to this campground. But I admit, my curiosity was piqued when I found, just as advertised, the oxblood, tepee-shaped tent draped in strands of yellow wild flowers. It was hard to miss.

The girl, now standing, still confused me. Elven ears, a green corset that hugged her small breasts into gentle protrusion. A green bikini bottom and pallid, freckled thighs decorated with some sort of dangling tinsel filament that shimmered in streaks of sunlight that sliced through seams in the canvas. And on top, an emerald tiara that kept together a nest of kinky, red hair spilling out in all directions. I was too afraid of her to wonder if I found her attractive.

The pixie put a kettle on a propane burner and flicked the flame to life. Within a minute the liquid hissed, filling the room with a pungent, fungal smell. She poured it into two cups. With the steaming liquid to my lips, I hesitated, my stomach dropping like a stone. The pixie noticed my trepidation and smiled, her lips curling upward like a demon, creases creeping too high. She sipped her tea and winked. So I sipped, too.

"I have an equation for the value of death. Do you want to hear it?" the pixie said.

I nodded.

"The weight of a death is inversely proportional to the wrongful acts of the individual. The greater the evil a person has done, the lower the societal death weight. More of a sliding scale than a straightforward equation," she said, taking another sip of her tea.

Her eyes probed me again, and I felt a burning sensation slide down my throat, and I thought of the time in high school when I'd made bacon while higher than a kite, and when the fat popped and splattered on my skin, I'd been convinced I was being burned alive. When I sobered, it felt silly, the little red pockmarks all but gone. I sipped again and waited.

"So Hitler was a one?" I said.

"Hitler was a zero. No registrable gravity. No sadness. Whoever killed him should bear no ill fate or karmic adversity."

"Probably quite the opposite. Karmic goodness."

"Still, it is not nothing to take a life," she said.

I nodded again, sipping my tea, feeling my head twirl slightly like an elevator slowing to a stop.

She beckoned me with her thin, pale finger accented by an oval turquoise ring.

"Now, who is it, and why do you feel they need to die?"

"You know, coming in here, seeing you—" I stopped and sipped the tea again while my heart rammed at the back of my throat. "I thought just now you were going to say something else. Like, you were going to be one of those all-life-is-sacred people." I let a slight chuckle loose, though nothing about this was funny. But based on her equation, she seemed to understand that a person could deserve to die. To need to die. That there were people who committed such egregious acts against the world, or an individual, or groups of individuals, who needed to be put down, and that society was better off for it. And she, I was hoping, would offer me the gift of an untraceable death. I tried to take another sip of my tea, but my tongue felt thick, coated with something herbaceous, delicious. My stomach warmed, and dots of sweat formed along my brow.

"I need to know that the person you intend to give this to deserves it. And that you deserve to give it to them. Taking a life puts you into a realm where the scale I described is not in your favor."

"But you don't understand. The things he's done to me," I said, watching the canvas of the tent beyond her start to move like ants in swirling lines.

"Then tell me. Tell me the who and their acts." She sat cross-legged on a cot. My body feeling heavy from the heat and the warmth of the tea, I sat on a cot opposite her.

"The person," I began, "is my business partner, Jackson Wright. And the reasons are myriad. For starters, he's fucking my wife and refuses to stop even though I've let him know I'm privy to it. Second, I am pretty sure he killed our third partner in a 'hunting accident' last year, over an argument regarding an account."

The pixie nodded, and I continued, filling her in on everything I'd found in evidence in detail. When I was done, I paused, breathed, and sipped my tea. I breathed deeply again, wiping my palms on my shorts again.

"I can help you," she said finally. "I do, on certain occasions, offer a traceless neurotoxin to people such as yourself. People who have become fearful, paranoid, alone in the trapped wasteland of their own minds. Lives of their own doing. Those deeply jaded souls ready to commit murder."

"I didn't *choose* this life. *They* did this to me. I just—I need your help. How much will it cost me? I must have it," I said, my chest constricting, tingling sensations down my back.

"You already *do* have it." Her smile lines deepened into jagged cuts. Raising my mug to look inside, my hands streaked with tracers, and the room spun in evil psychedelic circus images. "You've been drinking it in this whole time."

"But *you're* drinking the tea!" I said.

"It wasn't in the tea, it was a few drops of liquid at the bottom of your cup. The drink is just green tea and mushroom stems.

Lovely, isn't it? A spritely kick of caffeine with a microdose of psilocybin. It's quite an effective truth serum."

"You gave it to *me?*" I said, an acid rush hit my stomach, my heart gripped with electric pain.

"Sorry. You know, you really did have me figured out. I *do* think killing is wrong. All life *is* sacred. And by searching for death in a bottle, I knew it was a deserved death for you. You, sir, have the scales tipped far in your disfavor. Have you thought of this? That perhaps it is you who are standing in the way of love, of your partner's success. That just maybe, your partner killed in self-defense. Does he have a valid perspective different from your own? And this, maybe it is you who should die. You, a killer in your heart."

I had considered that the little pixie might be recording this, might find out who I was and extort money from me, but this? Delivering the poison to me, without even hearing me out first? Without understanding my why? And now, turning my pain, my suffering, my torment against me. I am *not* the villain in this story. I stood breathing deeply and counting to four. Box breathing. Closing my eyes, I tried to clear my head. When I opened them, the pixie's face came into focus, and I lunged for her, but she sidestepped me, and I crashed to the dirt floor.

Standing over me, she said, "You do anything to me, and you'll never find the antidote." The thought of an antidote hadn't yet crossed my mind, and a wrenching tightness in my chest loosened slightly. I *could* still live. I could balance my scales. I could do right. I brushed myself off and sat back on my cot.

"What do you want for the antidote?" I said. "I will give you any amount of money." And I would; I did quite well in my real estate investments with Jackson.

"First, you need to write a confession to Jackson and let him know what you were planning to do to him. I will keep the letter with me for safekeeping. If anything happens to me, it goes to the cops."

"Like, a real letter. Now?" I felt my head swirl with the psychedelic whoosh of the room.

"The effects you're feeling will wear off shortly—that's from the tea. The poison takes six hours. Well, closer to ten, but you won't be able to walk after six."

"What else? Money? What?"

"Second is, yes, money. I do have to maintain my laboratory. Ten thousand. Cash App. Now."

"And that's it?"

"Well, no. You also have to bring me another customer. Like Becca brought you to me. The woman who told you where to find me—yes, she had wanted to kill her mother. Can you believe that? Her own mother."

"Becca?" I clenched my eyes, remembering the girl in the boots and jean shorts. Was her name Becca? It was a blur now. I couldn't think straight. I was dying.

"You must continue the chain. I'll text you the geocache coordinates of the antidote once your link drinks the tea, just as you have." She took out a flip phone and typed something into it, then snapped it shut. "Becca will live, thanks to you. See, your scale is improving."

"But I have to find you another *victim?*"

"Victim." She wrinkled her nose. "That's not an accurate way to put it. I am protecting human lives, you see. From murder. Both yours and theirs. My scale is cleanly weighted in my favor. My karma stays even."

"Keep telling yourself that," I said, and regretted it. I needed the antidote and didn't want to fuck with my chances. "What if I can't find someone? What if time runs out?"

"Oh, I always stay at these festivals until the chain breaks, and it always breaks."

"You're fucking sick," I said, and her smile, impossibly, widened farther. "The chain breaks when someone is *murdered.*"

"You came to me to commit murder, and instead I have given you a choice. Make peace with your death or continue the chain. The next person you bring to me will deserve what they receive. Just as you have. The scale tips in your disfavor the moment you ask for the poison."

"A million. I will give you a million dollars. Cash. Now," I said.

"Time is running out. Go, find me someone. And who knows, perhaps the person you bring me might be your enemy. Perhaps you might save your own life twice today." She winked.

A cold chill rain down my arms. She was giving me a chance. It was fucked, but it was a chance. By killing me, she, in her twisted way, was setting me free. Her distorted little rendition of my situation replayed in my head. I *was* standing in the way of my business partner's love, *his* success, *his* dreams. Just by being alive—Jackson would gain full control of the company in my death, and I with his. He was a murderer already, though I couldn't prove it. But he would come here and ask for the poison. I knew that with absolute certainty.

All I had to do was plant the seed.

THE SPANISH SHAWL

by Michael Scott Moore

1997

Gray thick waves thump the morning beach. Robyn slips off her sweats. The sky's overcast, but she can tell from the warmish sand that the water won't be cold.

"Is it low tide?" she asks.

"Yeah," says Darren.

"Looks brutal," says Noah, and removes his glasses. He pulls down his own sweats and fits on a pair of swim fins from the DiMartinis' cabin. He has a lean, pale torso with little wrinkles at his abdomen, like the trunk of an aspen. His legs resemble strong branches under his floppy trunks, and Robyn likes his indolent, slack yellow hair.

"Storm's coming in," says Darren, squinting at the cloud cover.

They're just north of Point Mugu, an hour's drive from Calaveras Beach. The DiMartinis have an old cabin off Pacific Coast Highway, and the kids want to find a rock reef that's inaccessible from the road. Summer vacation started ten days ago.

Robyn and Darren, who are siblings, have been making this open-ocean swim since high school; Noah's never tried it before.

"We still need sunblock," Robyn says and tilts the bottle at Noah, as an offering. "UV rays don't care about clouds."

He submits while Robyn squeezes cream onto her fingers. Darren, with his dark fraternal eyes, watches her slide both hands across Noah's skin. The cream smells like shredded coconut.

"Want me to do you?" Noah says.

She steps in front of him, wordlessly, to face the water and submits to his long hands with a keen memory of last weekend.

"Follow us," she tells him when he's finished.

Robyn and Darren step backward into the water on squat fins. Robyn's aware of Noah's eyes on her torso but swivels her head to watch a wave rear up like a living thing. It spits and smacks the sand with *personality*, concentrated and thick, as if it wants to change the shape of the beach. She watches for her chance and dives before the next one hammers the sand. The white water churns. She's afraid of losing her snorkel and mask but finds a way under the turbulence to a calm spot beyond the waves where Darren's waiting already like a seal, watchful head bobbing at the surface.

She slicks back her hair. "Noah's nervous."

"I know," he says.

"It's funny, because he surfs."

Darren shrugs. "Not that well." He has thick shoulders and a level, thick-browed stare. He's spent a year of college as a fledgling Marine in the Reserve Officers' Training Corps. He doesn't smile at his sister. She finds it hard to read his gaze.

At last Noah struggles through the worst part of the turbulence and joins them, breathing hard.

"I'm not used to being out here without a board."

"It's different," Robyn agrees.

"Take your time," Darren tells him. "Don't get overwhelmed."

The idea of one or two hours in the water, far from the beach, without some kind of flotation device, can be a lot for a first-time ocean swimmer. Robyn smiles.

"Just breathe. When you find your rhythm, you'll be fine."

Noah nods with a lank smile that forms wrinkles at the edges of his mouth no different from the ones on his belly. He's awkward but masculine. He's grown from an excitable, towheaded kid into a tall, intelligent young man. Robyn doesn't mind. He's like a pane of glass she'd like to shatter.

The boys are freshmen; Robyn's a junior in marine science at UCLA. She has brown hair with bangs and a plump, tapered face which makes her look soft and kind; strangers are surprised to encounter a hard, quiet will. Their father has picked on Noah with jokes and acid remarks ever since his height crossed six feet. Ron DiMartini's a barrel-chested man of about five-six, with receding black hair and clever Italian eyes, and his rule of ridicule applies to Darren, too, especially since he started attending the gym at Middlebury. Robyn and her sister are exempt for some reason.

"Where's Darren? Where's your brother?" said their dad the other day by the pool.

"Not sure, why?" said Robyn.

"He needs to rake some leaves," said Ron.

"Want me to do it?" Robyn said.

"No, I want *him* to do it. I've asked him three or four times, the lazy son of a bitch."

Her father used to be a hippie, but he's become a blustering patriarch, fully suburbanized. Robyn thinks of his bluster as a kind of performance, no less than his long-haired bohemianism. Ron looks for strategies to cope with *his* father, Grandpa Frank, aged eighty-three, who wears a groomed mustache, expresses himself like a proud and vigorous rooster, and trims the lawn aboard a rattling tractor mower every weekend in Santa Rosa. Around him, Ron feels weak, Robyn thinks. Therefore he makes jokes about Darren.

"He's not queer, is he? We don't need a queer in the family."

"*Dad.*"

"Well, is he?"

"I don't know, you'll have to ask him."

Darren's never brought a girlfriend home, never mentioned a desire for any girl at Calaveras High as far as his sisters are concerned. Therefore, thinks Robyn, he surfs and lifts weights with Noah. Therefore, he joined ROTC. Therefore, come to think of it, this invitation to swim.

* * *

The boys race off, churning white water. She watches their legs and butts move like propeller screws. She's resisted sex with Noah so far. Robyn has an idea about love, that it will lift her out of her own boundaries like a tornado throwing Dorothy out of her shoes, and she prefers, for now, to remain in control.

She cleans her mask. At last she tongues her snorkel and swims after them. Swirls of sandy murk rise like dust storms from the ocean floor, and she glides over a cluster of boulders grown with fronds of kelp. She spots a blue, crescent-shaped slug with a ridge of yellow tendrils waving in the current. But she needs air before she investigates.

Darren's already at the surface, gazing down. When she pops her head up, he stops to raise his mask.

"What'd you find?" he says.

"A Spanish shawl."

"Oh!"

"On the rocks, straight down."

Darren nods and takes off his mask to polish it.

"We're swimming with the current right now," he says.

"Yeah, might be tough on the way back." She glances around. "Where's Noah?"

"Back there."

"You left him?"

"We raced a little."

"Is he still freaking out?"

"He'll be fine."

She makes a face. "You're not *both* joining the Marines, you know. He's a photographer."

"He'll be fine," repeats Darren, and replaces his mask.

She squints at the clouds. Darren nods at something behind her, and she turns to watch the approach of Noah's snorkel. He has nice form in the water—he keeps his arms inert by his side, which is unusual self-control for a beginner. Loose red swim trunks flower around his loins like a blood-colored jellyfish.

She taps his shoulder, and he pulls up his head to tread water.

"Hey."

"Doing better?"

"Yeah, you were right," he says. "Once you find a rhythm, you don't want to stop."

"You're not panicking?"

"Nah."

He smiles. She smiles. There's a not-uncomfortable silence.

"Right below us are some rocks," she says. "Wanna go down? I think I found a Spanish shawl."

"What's that?"

"A sea slug. I'll show you."

She sinks her snorkel underwater for a second to blow it clear. Then she nods at both boys like a rescue diver and plunges, turning a half somersault on the surface to make sure her bottom rises from the water so Noah can see.

* * *

The horns of its blue head move while the current stirs its ridge of feathery, orange-yellow tassels. It clings to a branch of kelp. The tassels are called cerata. Noah swims beside Robyn and reaches out to touch it, but she grabs his wrist. The slugs can be poisonous. He watches. Muscles under his ribs tense in the current, and from a distance, she hears high, faint song from a pod of dolphins.

Her body—their bodies — are bundles of warmth in the water. The Spanish shawl releases itself and starts to flip back and forth, head and tail flapping like a disembodied set of wings. Flamelike tassels wave. Robyn thinks of this beautiful creature, unscientifically, as an expression of helplessness—emotion to the ends of its colorful extremities—because she knows the flapping is not a way to swim so much as a sign of panic, a commitment to the wild currents. Maybe it's frightened by the presence of these swimming apes: Its little self feels overwhelmed.

Bubbles erupt from Noah's snorkel. They swim up through the silted water and take off their masks.

"I've never seen anything like that," he says, and laughs.

"Isn't it great?"

"I wish I had a camera." His face looks wild and alive. "I had no idea these things existed."

"You'll see more if you keep doing it." She smiles. "They're common, if you know where to look."

They tread water. A light, warm breeze blows across the water, and Robyn has an urge to move closer to him. Then her brother lifts his head about five yards away.

"Hey, weirdo," Robyn says.

"I heard dolphins."

"Same here. Did you see them?" she says.

"They're a ways off," Darren answers.

"Wait, did *I* hear dolphins?" Noah says. "What do they sound like?"

"Clicks and shrieks."

"Not very loud," says Darren.

"They were talking about you," Robyn says, and splashes Noah's face. He splashes back, and Darren watches them play fight with inexpressive eyes. The leaden clouds break apart for a moment and reveal a streak of shameless light above the beach.

"We're close to the sea lion colony," Darren says.

"Can't wait," says Noah.

"Just be careful, they're territorial."

Darren turns to paddle ahead. Noah follows. Robyn watches them and resettles her mask.

The ocean floor spills down through greenish murk. A pile of rocks rises up in its place to form a reef, and a forest of seaweed sways like palm fronds in a slow wind. Little fish cross under their masks in formation, and Darren dives through them, forcing part of the school to scatter. They reform and keep moving in massive swirls, like a cloud of starlings.

Robyn returns to the surface, where Noah has his mask in the water.

"You don't want to dive?" she says.

"I'll stay up where I can breathe."

"Okay."

Darren swims up for air, and Robyn returns to a depth of ten or fifteen feet to watch sea lions hunt among the rocks. One steers through the fish, darting left and right, hoping for a meal. But the fish maintain a constant margin of nine inches on every side, as if they can feel the predator's heat. The sea lion spots Robyn and darts at her as a warning, which makes her startle, and she hears a splash overhead: Noah, thrashing in sympathetic surprise.

She glances up. Darren's treading water beside him. All Robyn can see are their torsos and cycling legs, but as she floats to the top she happens to notice Darren's hand move for Noah's trunks. The back of his hand grazes Noah's crotch, not by mistake. Noah thrashes again, swirling his limbs in a fresh cloud of foam.

At the surface he looks confused more than upset. Darren wears a wicked grin.

"Sorry man," he says.

"What the *hell*," says Noah.

Robyn blinks.

"Everything okay?" she asks.

"Fine," says Noah.

But she snorts in flat rejection of his answer, startled by the violence in her blood. What Robyn just saw feels more unusual than any of the morning's natural wonders. She pretends to clear her snorkel and resists an urge to dart at her brother like a territorial sea lion.

* * *

"That was great," says Noah on the beach.

Which part? Robyn wants to say.

"Next time I'll bring my camera."

Same here, she thinks on their way across the beach. *Take some candids.*

A warm summer breeze has started to push onshore. During the last part of the swim, they had to fight a rip current through the surf, so they're all out of breath. Both boys have a residue of salt on their shoulders, and a stranger watching them might think Robyn was the essential female at the center of a triangle. But that's not how she feels.

The DiMartinis' shack stands at the foot of a billboard on Pacific Coast Highway. Their parents lease the cabin from the owner of a seaside ranch, which is the sort of property that used to be common in this neighborhood north of Malibu. The cabin's small—a former tackle shed. But it has a kitchen with a fridge and a stove. They keep snorkel and fishing gear in a locked closet, two old surfboards, but not much else.

"We forgot to get beer from the car," says Darren.

"It's too early for beer," says Robyn.

"One won't hurt," says Noah. "Will it?"

Darren wanders down to the car, which is parked on a long gravel driveway indistinguishable from a country road. Robyn opens the shack and sits with Noah on an L-shaped couch near a window. The whole shack has an odor of dust and horses and mold. There's a corral with live horses visible from the window, through some eucalyptus and Scotch pine.

"Have fun?" Robyn says.

Noah nods, and she wants to ask what happened in the water, but everything's too fresh. Her brother's gay? And Noah's bi? Or what exactly's going on? This morning she wanted a relationship with him, but not if he has a relationship with Darren, holy hell.

"I think I *do* need a beer," she says, and touches a sore muscle in her left shoulder, raises the arm to check for more pain, winces, and finally moves it in a wide circle, flamboyantly.

"Hurt?" says Noah.

"Stiff."

"Want a massage?" he offers, and Robyn studies his face, which is earnest, uncertain, fine boned, and androgynous behind his glasses. The androgyny is one reason she wants him. Oh dear God.

"Maybe just my shoulders," she says, and sits in front of him.

While his hands begin to work, she regrets it, because a brother who's gay and not out to his sister might also be a brother who's vulnerable.

But she doesn't move. Instead she remains on the cold floor with her eyes closed, dreaming in pleasure under Noah's attention, like a house cat, until Darren barges through the door and sets down a Coleman cooler with a clank.

"It's starting to rain," he says.

"Fuck," says Robyn, who would rather not drive home in bad weather.

"Yeah, it looks serious. The clouds are dark."

Darren, all business, distributes beer and sits close to Robyn on the floor, wearing cargo shorts and a red ROTC shirt. His eyes are moody and Mediterranean, to balance his smile, which can be flashy and bright.

They clink bottles. Darren tilts his up with a defiant look. This bitchy insistence on drinking, Robyn thinks, is new since college.

"Stiff," she tells him by way of explanation.

"We swam a lot today," adds Noah.

"I was there," says Darren.

He reaches up to the kitchen counter, behind him, to switch on an old CD player. It's loaded with Metallica from a previous visit. Robyn doesn't like her brother's taste in music, but Noah runs a thumb into a tight fiber of her trapezius, and her vision blurs.

"How long have you guys had this cabin?" says Noah.

"I don't know, almost twenty years?" Darren says. "The rent's dirt cheap."

"Your dad found it?"

"Yeah, through some hippie friends, in the late seventies, I think. The ranch owner here knew Neil Young. You know that album *Zuma?*"

"Sure."

"Recorded nearby."

Robyn stares at Darren through a faint haze and tries to picture Neil Young against the backdrop of this horse-and-ocean landscape—the high palm trees, the brush-grown highway, the gas stations like country stores. She finds that all she has to do in her imagination is remove some expensive cars.

"This shack," she tells them, "is the reason I wanted to become a marine biologist. We don't have rock reefs in Calaveras Beach."

"Nope," says Darren.

"I guess not," says Noah. "The bottom's all sand."

Robyn flexes her shoulders and glances up. "I've thought about living here, like when I have a field project in grad school? Wouldn't that be great?"

Darren stares at the floor and nods. She realizes too late that it might be a sensitive topic: Robyn, the overachieving older sister. While Darren seems unsure of his future in college.

"Be a shame to give it up," he says.

Outside, a soft rain starts to patter the trees.

"You have a major yet?" says Noah, sensing the drift of conversation.

"Sure," says Darren. "History."

"Plus the Marines," Noah points out, and Darren shrugs.

"Just pursuing my interests."

"You're both freshmen," says Robyn. "You don't need to have everything nailed down."

Noah's not just a photographer; he wants to be a poet. Or, he is a poet. Or, he aspires to a poetical career.

"What's *your* plan?" Darren snaps, and Noah lets go of Robyn's shoulders to pick up his beer. He squeezes one eye shut to stare, theatrically, down its neck, then drinks.

He says: "I want to graduate with honors from Hunter and ride to Mongolia on a giraffe."

"Fieldwork," says Robyn.

"Maybe I can live here while I do it."

"Long commute," says Darren.

"Especially on a giraffe," says Robyn, but notes in silence that Noah has suggested living with her after college.

"Dad won't like it," Darren says.

Robyn looks up. "Yeah, he doesn't like you anymore."

"Right, what happened?" says Noah. "He liked me well enough when we were kids."

"You got tall," Robyn says. "And you grew your hair. He thinks you're a hippie now."

"He says you're a bad influence," Darren says.

"On *you?*" says Noah with unexpected force.

"Our dad's changed," Robyn says to make peace.

"Why, do you think?" Noah asks.

"Because of us," Robyn says. "Kids are expensive."

Darren shrugs. It's not quite a satisfying answer. But the conversation puts Robyn in the strange position of defending their dad, and maybe she understands him better than her siblings because she had to negotiate on her own with both parents for the first two years of her life. But Darren can also be a moralist: He has some of their dad's rigid habits of thought. At the same time, and for the same reason, he fights with Ron over every fucking topic on TV.

"He's been an activist all his life," says Darren.

"That's true," Robyn says. "He needs a banner to fly."

"When he was young, he read a lot about the JFK assassination, which made him curious about conspiracies," Darren says. "Now he thinks the Clintons are killers."

"He wants a solid answer for everything," Robyn says, glancing up. "Which might be why he's against you—you're hard to read."

No one says a word. They listen to rain fall on the trees, on the beach parking lot, and on the soil of the ranch. The beer in her blood and the proximity of Noah's legs make Robyn's barriers tremble.

"Where's your bathroom?" he says.

"Right there."

Darren points at a door facing a wooden ladder, which leads up to the loft. Noah extricates himself and stands. They watch him close the hollow, ill-hung door. Cool, fresh air stirs through the window just from the force of the rain.

"Storm's here," Darren says.

"The ride home's gonna suck," she says.

"I can drive," he offers.

"Maybe we should just stay over."

"You think so?"

"It's a thought," she says to make it sound casual, but the cabin has only two beds—the loft at the top of the ladder, and this L-shaped couch.

"You'd like that," he says after a moment, and she stares at her brother with round, curious, imploring eyes. *Don't make this weird.*

"Meaning what," she says.

"You're just getting along," he suggests.

The hollow door fails to muffle the sound of Noah's urination. The streaming raises a wave of embarrassment. Robyn wonders if Darren's acting nasty on purpose. She takes a swallow of beer.

"Dad thinks you're gay," she announces, and Darren halts his own bottle halfway to his mouth to punish her with his eyes. The bathroom door opens with a scrape. Noah emerges to the sound of the toilet.

"Hey. Sorry," he says, and returns to his place on the couch.

"Maybe I am," Darren says, not without haughtiness or rage, aimed laser-like at his sister.

"Maybe you're what?" says Noah.

"Gay."

"Oh?"

"What do *you* think?" Darren asks.

Robyn gives a sudden smile and turns to look at Noah. From the look on his face she can tell he's mortified. But he's also in the process of nodding like a straight dude, pretending to be surprised.

"Fine by me," he says.

"*Is* it?" says Darren.

"I mean, it's nobody's business."

"Not if you don't want it to be," says Darren with a sarcastic smile.

The rain in the trees begins to roar. On the wild-grown soil of the ranch, it raises a smell of horses and jasmine. Robyn twists her body to stare at Noah, alarmed and alert, hoping for more information, then lets out a derisive laugh.

"I have no idea what just happened," she says.

"Sure you do," says Darren.

* * *

The storm sends detonations of thunder and quiet flashes of lightning from over the Pacific. They reload the car under a warm rain. There's an electric profusion of smells, from ozone to mud, and the afternoon feels explosive with spring.

Robyn sits in the passenger seat with her hair straggling and wet, though it's clear that Noah wants her to sit in back with him. Darren pulls the Nissan out to PCH, and she snaps the levers of the old heater to one side and cranks the fan. At last she turns to Noah, who's wet as a dog.

"Okay?" she says.

"Fine."

He takes off his glasses to polish them. Smooth as Cary Grant, she thinks with sarcasm. Darren accelerates down the highway and switches on some horrible CD. Robyn has spent most of the afternoon resentful of her brother, but now her panicked mind turns on Noah and blames him for everything. She feels so much desire and so much affection and she wants it all to move with so much fervor toward his dark and thoughtful voice, the calm precision of his hands. But he's wrecked it now, hasn't he? Both of them. Somehow. Her thoughts flutter back and forth like a sea slug. She can't contain her mind any more than she can arrive at a serious assessment of the day.

But *she* brought it up. She elicited this information.

She rolls down her window.

"What are you doing?" says Darren. "You just turned on the heat."

The window lets in the odors of jasmine and lightning and mud. She likes it. She opens the glove compartment.

"Does Dad have cigarettes?"

"Dad hasn't smoked in years."

"I thought he had some left over."

"You're trying to smoke *now*?" says Darren.

"She's out of control," says Noah with a smirk.

"Shut up," she says. "Both of you," and slams the compartment shut.

Her brother turns up the music. Robyn switches off the heat but cranks the volume. "Is *this* what you want?" she says, and while they speed along the highway to the thump of Judas Priest, she has to pull her wet and windblown hair from her eyes, from her cheeks, over and over, out of petulance as well as defiance. Revulsion and desire can live in a single heart. "Robyn, shut the window," say the boys, but she won't.

MRS. A

by Kendall Brunson

Mrs. Abernathy stood by the sliding glass doors, studying the violent waves toppling and crashing over each other. A strong wind blew sand off the dunes. She hated the surf and the sand now. She couldn't even remember the last time she'd been for a walk on the beach. Not since... Mrs. Abernathy refused to think about it.

"Mother, are you listening?" her son asked on the other line.

"Of course I am listening, Peter. Apparently you aren't, though. You don't hear me when I say I don't like the new girl."

Peter sighed. He sounded exactly like his father. If it didn't annoy Mrs. Abernathy so much, she might find it endearing. "Chrissy is not new. She's been with you for months now."

"My point exactly. She still uses too much detergent in the laundry and slathers mayo on my tuna, no matter how much I explain. It's not rocket science, Peter. It's tuna fish. You wouldn't have to guess if you came to visit. Yesterday, she cranked the air conditioning down to seventy-four. *Seventy-four.* As though she's the one paying for it. Are you writing this down?"

"Of course," he said, though she didn't believe him. "Is that everything?"

"If you want me to go on, I can. She won't shut up about this new boyfriend of hers, and she takes too long with her chores now. I swear, I don't understand why you insist upon this *help*. I'm as sharp as a tack."

"You fell, Mother. Actually, no, you've *fallen* multiple times. I just want someone there checking in on you, especially since you refuse to move to the city. Megan and I would love for you to be closer to us. You could see the grandkids more often. There are some excellent condos close by. Even older communities—"

"Pssh." Mrs. Abernathy dismissed this. She refused to be stuck in a condo. Or even worse, in an apartment surrounded by a bunch of old people. Yes, okay, so she had fallen a few times, but to her credit, she hadn't broken or sprained anything. She was, in her old age, excellent at falling. She regretted even telling her son at all.

"Are you sure you like living at the beach still? After everything?"

Now it was Mrs. Abernathy's turn to sigh. "Please, Peter."

"Okay, okay," her son said, relenting. "I need to get back on the bench. I'll call the service tomorrow and ask for someone new."

Peter was a federal judge. If only his father had been here to see his son become a fourth-generation lawyer and now judge. She knew her son's days were long, that he often went into the office early and stayed late—unlike his lazy counterparts—which meant he and that wife of his, who for some reason also insisted upon working, had nannies to make sure the children got where they needed to go. Her son lived on the edge of exhaustion, though Mrs. Abernathy didn't think it was right they had waited so long to have children. It was their own fault for being so tired, really. "You do that," Mrs. Abernathy said, and hung up the phone.

She returned to the bills and heard Chrissy clomping around upstairs. The girl was polite, if a little stupid. Said *please*, *thank you*, and *ma'am*. Mrs. Abernathy thought she could work with stupid, but she'd had her fill.

Chrissy came downstairs. "Take your lunch outside today?" Chrissy's top was too tight around the waist. Didn't her son pay the girl thirty dollars an hour? That was surely enough money to at least buy a pair of scrubs that fit correctly.

"When I'm done with the bills." Mrs. Abernathy readjusted her glasses and sliced open the Visa bill with the metal letter opener.

"That looks pretty sharp," Chrissy said, inspecting the dagger in Mrs. Abernathy's hand.

Mrs. Abernathy held it up to the light. It was heavy brass encrusted with jewels and ornate detailing. It was still so sharp and pointed that she stored it in the matching sheath. "Mr. Abernathy purchased this for me on our honeymoon in Morocco."

Mr. Abernathy had given her a present every day of their monthlong trip from Spain to Portugal and then finally Morocco. In addition to the letter opener, he gifted her ruby earrings, two gold bracelets with a matching necklace, pearl earrings, a sapphire ring... She stopped going through the list. It didn't matter anyway. Everything was gone now, except for this letter opener.

"Wow. Morocco. Is that, like, in Europe?"

What were they teaching children these days? "No, dear. Africa."

Chrissy's eyes widened so she looked like one of those awful cartoon characters the kids loved when they were little. "Wow. Furthest I've been is to visit my cousin in Nashville, and a stop in Dollywood."

Mrs. Abernathy gave a tight smile and decided not to correct the girl on the use of *further* versus *farther*. "I'm hungry now. Please bring lunch out to the veranda."

"Sure thing," Chrissy said and disappeared into the kitchen.

"Light on the mayo," Mrs. Abernathy called after the girl, but her instructions felt hopeless.

Mrs. Abernathy tucked the letter opener in the casing and set it down on the desk. Then she took the Visa bill, red pen, and receipts outside. The ocean roared. A storm brewed off the coast in the Atlantic. Dense, black rain clouds threatened to move west. Still, there looked to be just enough time to eat a proper lunch outside.

She tried to ignore the homes flanking the Cape Cod–style beach house with its wooden shingles and original single-pane windows. The new monstrosities were all concrete and reinforced glass. Mr. Abernathy would have hated it. Frankly, part of her was glad he wasn't here to see it. His family's home had been on the island for over a hundred years, long before beach living became fashionable. They used to live full-time in Jacksonville and then spend summers on the island, but after Mr. Abernathy's death, Mrs. Abernathy couldn't continue in the city. It became too painful to see the memories of her husband everywhere. After moving to the island, her daughter began her downward spiral that ended with... Mrs. Abernathy didn't want to think about that either. She wished the ocean was loud enough to drown out her thoughts.

Chrissy set lunch on the table. Mrs. Abernathy had eaten the same lunch every day since she and Mr. Abernathy returned home from their honeymoon—with the exception of eating lunch at the club. If not, it was always one can of tuna with a dash of mayo, relish, and salt, no pepper, and ten Pepperidge Farm wheat crackers on the side.

Per usual, Chrissy applied the mayo generously. Mrs. Abernathy considered saying something, but the girl would be gone soon.

"Whatcha doing?" Chrissy asked. Couldn't this girl say anything correctly?

"I'm reviewing my credit card statement."

"You go line by line like that?"

Mrs. Abernathy looked down at the red pen marks, where she matched each purchase with a receipt from the envelope. "Of course, don't you?"

Chrissy shrugged. "Not really."

"How do you know you're not being taken advantage of? That a waiter didn't leave themselves an overly generous tip? Or that your credit card information hasn't been stolen?"

The girl pursed her lips. "Dunno. Just kind of assume it's right."

"Well, you know what they say about assumptions."

"No?"

"Well, I don't like to be vulgar before I eat." Mrs. Abernathy pulled the plate toward her. "If you please."

But Chrissy didn't take the hint. Instead, she pulled out her phone and plopped down on the chair right next to her. Mrs. Abernathy swore she felt the deck shake a little. If not for the girl being let go, Peter would be paying to replace the piers.

"You should be more careful with your money. Or else it won't go as far," Mrs. Abernathy said.

"Eh, not like there's much to lose." Then the girl sent a text. Her fingers moved much like Alice's had. Her daughter had always been on the phone.

"My father used to say that good decisions now lead to good options down the road," Mrs. Abernathy said.

"I didn't have a dad. At least, not a good one."

Mrs. Abernathy let out a huff of air but restrained herself from saying *obviously*. Chrissy was prone to making odd and awkward remarks. Mrs. Abernathy studied her. Now that she was eighty, everyone looked young, so it was difficult to judge ages, but the girl was probably in her twenties or thirties. Pretty, even if she was a little fat. There was a regalness to her though. A sharp nose, good chin, and long neck. *Just like Alice.* There was some potential underneath the mess.

"Are you from the island?" Mrs. Abernathy asked. She realized she knew very little about the girl.

"Yep. Born and raised."

"That's nice. I wanted my children to be brought up here, but Mr. Abernathy's work kept us in the city. Still, we came every chance we could."

Chrissy shrugged. "It's overrated. And crazy expensive. I rent a studio and it's two grand. Me and my boyfriend have a plan though."

Mrs. Abernathy did the polite thing and nodded. What could she say to someone so blatantly bad with money? Spending that on a studio apartment? It better look like the Ritz inside. "That's why it's more important than ever to be careful with your money."

"I invest when I can."

"Do you now? Isn't that good. May I ask what in? Apple's a solid investment. As well as Microsoft. Mr. Abernathy did very well with Microsoft. He invested early."

"Crypto," the girl said. "My boyfriend got me into it. He's real good at that stuff. Watches all these YouTube videos about it."

Her sentence structure was like listening to metal grating, but Mrs. Abernathy was more concerned about the mention of crypto. "My daughter invested and *lost* a lot of money, also encouraged by a boyfriend. She had a tendency of throwing good money after bad. I'd hate to see that happen to you."

"It won't, Mrs. A."

Mrs. Abernathy did not appreciate her name being shortened to a single letter. "That's what Alice always said. She was sure until she wasn't. My Alice, she was…" The words were stuck in her throat, and Mrs. Abernathy lifted a napkin and dabbed at her eyes.

This was why she didn't talk about her daughter, but someone needed to warn this girl.

"You okay? I'm real sorry. Didn't mean to upset you."

This girl had some nerve. "Yes, of course I am okay," Mrs. Abernathy snapped.

Then, oddly, the girl began to cry. Mrs. Abernathy didn't know what to do. She'd never been very good at the motherly stuff. Wasn't that what Alice had accused her of constantly, being a terrible mother? What were the last words she called her, an "evil bitch"? Mrs. Abernathy pushed the thought away. "This is very inappropriate at work."

Chrissy used her entire arm as a rag to wipe her nose. Mrs. Abernathy tried to suppress a shudder. The girl's phone dinged, and Chrissy craned her neck to look down the beach. Then she typed something. "I'm gonna take my break. Be back soon, Mrs. A."

As the girl stepped off the veranda and onto the long decking that lead out to the beach, Mrs. Abernathy swore she felt the piers shake again. She ignored her lunch and studied Chrissy from afar. She could see her terrible posture from a distance and made a mental note to remind the girl about this before she left for the day.

A man met her on the sand. He was short, Chrissy's height. She clearly knew him because soon they were arguing. Her arms were crossed while he pointed his finger at her face. Mrs. Abernathy wished she could hear the fight, but the waves and winds squashed any hope of that. Then, the man looked over at Mrs. Abernathy, and they locked eyes across the dunes and seagrass. His dark glare sent a shiver through her, but then his gaze was back to Chrissy, who looked like she was saying no.

Chrissy turned to leave, but the man grabbed her and shook her. Chrissy freed herself from his grasp and ran back toward the house. Mrs. Abernathy had no intention of making it known she had seen such a disgusting display. That poor girl. She knew how it felt, the humiliation of being spoken to that way, touched that way, even if it was only temporary. Mr. Abernathy had never touched her like that, but Alice, on the other hand. Well, the less said, the better.

She took her plate inside before Chrissy walked back. From the kitchen, she saw the girl slump onto the chair outside, her face in her hands.

She felt a little sorry for the girl, but somehow she had become the girl's caretaker instead of the other way around. How had her son found this Chrissy? Peter said he used a service. "They're the best in town, Mother." The best in town? Ha. She could call the service and ask for a new girl immediately. She would, of course, give Chrissy a kind, but honest assessment. She didn't want to impede her ability to work, but this was a little ridiculous. Fighting with a boyfriend outside of the workplace and crying? Not to mention everything else? Mrs. Abernathy wanted her gone now. Surely, this kind, sobbing, stupid girl could not be the best the service had to offer, and if so, well, no thank you.

She noted Chrissy's purse on the counter—a giant, black, frayed faux-leather monstrosity. Maybe that would have information about the company she worked for. She checked over her shoulder. Chrissy was still crying on the veranda. Mrs.

Abernathy felt a quick thrill. How long had it been since she'd snooped? She used to read her daughter's diary entries when she was younger, which were quite benign. Peter had been more difficult to spy on. She'd only come across a condom when he was home from college and two beer cans in the back of his car. He had received a stern talking-to, which put an end to that. He was always such a good boy. After Alice dropped out of college, the real trouble began. There was so much pot, to the point where Mr. Abernathy insisted on sending her to treatment. That only made things worse, especially after he died.

Mrs. Abernathy had hoped moving to the beach house would improve Alice's temperament after Mr. Abernathy's death, get her away from the bad influences in the city. But Mrs. Abernathy would soon learn there were bad influences everywhere. On the island, there was a decades-long loop of Alice coming and going. Getting better and then disappearing—sometimes for years on end. Promising to do better. Sometimes, there'd been slivers of hope, but the last time had been different. The stealing. The drugs. The gun. *The gun.*

Mrs. Abernathy forced herself to focus on the task at hand. Chrissy's handbag was filled with junk, crumpled receipts, open tubes of lipstick she clearly never wore. She let out a gasp and pulled a long, curved brass letter opener from the purse, still encrusted with small jewels. It was the very last item she had left that she felt tied her to Mr. Abernathy, and here it was, in this blubbering idiot girl's filthy purse, tossed in like loose change.

"Mrs. A?"

Mrs. Abernathy turned around to see the girl claiming to be Chrissy walking toward her, slack-jawed by what she saw Mrs. Abernathy doing.

"What are you doing?" Chrissy said. Her eyes were that of a child's, caught in the act. Worse, no, they were those of her daughter. Someone who knew they'd been caught but was desperately trying to hide the truth. "You can't do that."

Mrs. Abernathy held up the letter opener, still in its sheath. "Why do you have this?" She felt stupid for asking the question. Chrissy, to her knowledge, had never taken anything else. Had she overheard her call with Peter? Was she after revenge for being let go?

The girl wouldn't meet her eyes. "I thought he'd be happy with it. It seems like it's worth a lot."

"That who would be happy with it?" The fact that this *thief* required her to pull teeth for information was somehow more insulting. The girl refused to answer; instead, she kept her eyes lowered. "I think you need to leave, now," Mrs. Abernathy said, and slipped the letter opener into her pocket.

The girl, panicked, walked toward her. "I can't do that. Not yet."

Mrs. Abernathy looked for the phone, but it wasn't back in the charger. She'd just been talking to Peter. Where had she set it down? She saw it on the kitchen counter, but so did Chrissy. Faster and younger, Chrissy hurried to the phone and tossed it across the room. The cheap, black plastic splintered on the parquet floors. "I'm sorry, Mrs. A. This will be over real quick if you just tell me where it is."

"Where what is?"

"The ring. The blue one."

Mrs. Abernathy felt a chill run through her. "How do you know about the sapphire?" The sapphire ring, flanked by two diamonds, had been the first gift on the honeymoon. Mr. Abernathy told her the ring represented their new family. When Alice was a girl, Mrs. Abernathy had promised it would one day be hers. Their last interaction had been over this very ring. When Alice demanded she hand over the ring, Mrs. Abernathy refused. That's when Alice pulled out the gun and pointed it at her face. "I'm in trouble, Mom. They're going to kill me. You have to help me." But Alice was always in trouble. She always owed some debt. Was always sneaking into the house and leaving with something she could trade away. Before Mrs. Abernathy realized it, Alice had cleaned her of every single gift from her honeymoon, except for the ring and the letter opener. Alice had pawned everything else. "They're going to kill me." How could Mrs. Abernathy know that this time she meant it? "You evil bitch."

The last time she saw Alice was at the morgue to identify her. When she closed her eyes, Mrs. Abernathy could still picture her daughter's face. The void in her skull, her hair caked in blood and sand. They'd found her body in the dunes less than a mile from her home. The police suspected Alice had been killed shortly after leaving her mother's house that last time.

Chrissy's face was blotchy and puffy. "I know you've still got it. I can't leave here without it. Not again."

There was that thrumming in her temples again. Just like the last time she fell. Mrs. Abernathy turned, but there was the step from the kitchen up to the living room. The edge of her toe caught on the stair, and she plunged forward. Her knee slammed into the hard wooden step. Pain split her open. She howled.

Chrissy knelt down in front of her. She was also crying. Why was this stupid, stupid girl crying when she was the one in pain?

"Where is it, Mrs. A? Where's the ring?" Chrissy said in a pleading tone. "You have to tell me.".

But Mrs. Abernathy couldn't answer her. The pain was so sharp that she was afraid she might pass out.

"Hey there, Marilyn."

Mrs. Abernathy looked up to see a man leaning on a wooden pillar that separated the kitchen from the formal dining room. It was the man Chrissy had been fighting with on the beach. Now in her home, Mrs. Abernathy finally recognized him—Judd. An insipid name for a boy. Everything about him still looked like it was on the wrong body. He was short with long arms. Slightly pudgy in the neck and torso with pin-straight legs. Thin lips and narrow eyes on a wide face. Like a Mr. Potato Head that had been assembled wrong. Somehow, Alice had claimed to have loved him. Mrs. Abernathy had only met him one other time, when she found the pair rifling through her jewelry box. Alice had tried to play it off, but Mrs. Abernathy could see the hunger in her daughter's eyes. Hunger for something so much deeper than food. Her beautiful, vivacious daughter, the daughter who won the school spelling bee in the sixth grade, who did a summer abroad in Arles and painted postcards imitating Van Gogh to mail back to her parents and brother, who got into Brown—just like her father—*her* daughter was reduced to a gaunt, petty thief. Though there was nothing petty about stealing three-carat diamond studs. Mrs. Abernathy had warned Alice that if she ever brought him back, she would call the cops. "I love him." She wasn't sure her daughter could remember real love, not anymore.

"I've got this," Chrissy said to Judd, almost breathless.

Judd walked toward Chrissy. "Obviously not," he said, and Mrs. Abernathy was shocked when he shoved Chrissy. Instinctively, the girl swung her arms around her stomach, rolling into a ball, protecting what truly mattered. The puzzle piece slid into place. The tight shirt. The shaking piers. The overuse of mayo. Chrissy was pregnant.

Judd bent down and grabbed Mrs. Abernathy by the shoulders. "Where's the ring, Marilyn?"

Mrs. Abernathy forced herself not to cry out from the pain in her knee and Judd's strong grip. "I don't have it."

"Bullshit. It was Alice's ring, and you stole it."

There was no stealing what was hers. "I said I don't have it."

He turned to Chrissy, who was trying to stand. Her bump was small, barely noticeable, but now with her hand resting on her stomach, Mrs. Abernathy could see it clearly.

"Go look upstairs," Judd said.

"I've looked everywhere. I really have."

He locked his cold eyes on Mrs. Abernathy but talked to Chrissy. "Go look again. Me and Marilyn are going to have a little chat, and if you don't find that ring..."

"But—"

"Go!" The house shook with his command.

Chrissy raced up the stairs, well, as much as the girl could race. A slight hustle was the better description. It made sense now. Mrs. Abernathy hadn't concerned herself with Chrissy slowing down, taking so long to sort the laundry or clean, because there was nothing left to steal, not of any real value. Yes, there were still some rare books in the library, a very expensive first edition of Poe's *Tales* as well as a beautiful, illustrated edition of *Jane Eyre* that could fetch a nice sum, but so few people understood the value of books these days. She never worried about them disappearing.

Judd left Mrs. Abernathy on the floor and began to pace.

"When did you get back in town?" she asked. She had, of course, told the police about him, but she'd been informed that he'd skipped town.

He smiled in the sort of menacing way that reminded her of a Hitchcock movie. Mr. Abernathy loved those. "Eh, a few months ago. I swung by to see what you're up to and saw Chrissy leaving your house." Her stomach turned, thinking how he had targeted that poor girl. He continued, "God, she was easy. So was Alice. You know, Alice would have been fine if you'd just given her the stupid fucking ring."

Outside, the dark, ominous storm moved like a wall of doom over the house.

"It was you," she said, and used her elbows to prop herself up.

Judd didn't flinch from the accusation. "No, I loved her. She told you she was in trouble. She needed help. She needed that fucking ring. What does an old bitch like you need with a ring like that when you're so close to rotting in the ground anyway?"

This was the sort of man Alice fell for? Mrs. Abernathy had raised her daughter to look for quality men, but as though to thumb her nose at her mother at every turn, Alice had dated worse and worse men until she picked this trash off the ground.

"If you knew she was in trouble, why didn't you get her the money? If you're truly a man, then you would act like one."

He flinched now, unable to stand his manhood being challenged. "What the fuck did you say to me?" Judd reached for his waistband and pulled out a gun.

It looked exactly like the one her daughter had pointed at her. Her beautiful fallen daughter. "Mom, just tell me," she'd begged through tears, pointing the gun at her mother. Mrs. Abernathy had cried too. Out of fear, yes. But also out of deep and utter heartbreak for her daughter. She should have given Alice the ring, she knew that now. In her dreams, she gave her the ring over and over and over again. She would sell her house and every worldly possession to give Alice whatever money she claimed to need. Peter had consoled her. He hadn't blamed her. Mrs. Abernathy had been just trying to set boundaries and not allow Alice to walk all over her. She wished she had. She didn't need the ring, or the house, or the money. It was all useless to her. Especially now.

Mrs. Abernathy closed her eyes and pictured Alice. She'd been shot in the head, between the eyes. She'd known what was coming. That's what the detective had said. Instantly, Mrs. Abernathy was back in the coroner's office. They'd asked if she wanted to call her son to identify Alice, but Mrs. Abernathy had less life to live. She didn't want Peter to carry that visual around with him for the rest of his life. It had been her who caused this after all.

She opened her eyes again and looked up over the barrel of the gun. "I said if you were truly a man, then you would act like one. If Alice needed the money, you would have provided."

Judd glowered at her, and she thought he might just shoot her then. She was still of some use to him, so he lowered the gun and walked over to the stairs. "Hurry the fuck up," he called up to Chrissy.

She knew this was not the time to point out his overreliance on the words *fuck* and *fucking*, but it really did make him sound far less intelligent than he was. "So what's the big plan, then, after you get the ring and kill me?"

"Moving to Mexicana. Ain't that right, babe?" he called up the stairs. Chrissy walked down, shaking her head. "Fuck. Fuck!" Judd exclaimed.

"You can kill me now, but you'll never find the ring."

Chrissy looked panicked. "We're not gonna hurt you. Right, Judd?"

"It's fine," Judd said, ignoring her question. "We'll be living large. Who cares what happens to her?"

Clearly, this was not what Chrissy had signed up for.

Mrs. Abernathy needed to make sure the girl fully understand. "He dated my daughter. Did he tell you that? Right before he killed her."

Judging by the horrified expression on the girl's face, this was news to her too.

"I said I *didn't* kill her," he seethed.

"Are your crypto investments not working out as you hoped?" Mrs. Abernathy asked Judd. His nostrils flared, and he looked at Chrissy, who refused to meet his eyes. "He did the same thing to my daughter. He took her money, sunk it in bad investments. He convinced her to steal from me, and it didn't work out for her either." This girl was stupid, but she didn't deserve to pay for it with her life. Mrs. Abernathy couldn't let that happen again.

"She would have been fine if you hadn't been a selfish bitch and just given her the ring."

Chrissy stepped between them, trying to be the peacekeeper. "Please, Mrs. A. We'll leave. I swear, and you'll never hear from us again. We won't hurt you if you just tell us where the ring is. Then we can leave the country."

This girl believed the words coming out of her mouth. Mrs. Abernathy had seen this very look on her daughter's face countless times.

"I can't do that," Mrs. Abernathy said. "I can't give you the ring. I've already told you, I don't have it."

"See? Told you, she's a lying bitch. Alice showed me pictures. She'd rather have her own kid shot between the fucking eyes than give up any of her precious bullshit crap."

Mrs. Abernathy felt swimmy again. Luckily, she was already on the ground.

"How do you know Alice was shot between the eyes?"

Judd blinked rapidly, as though moving his eyes quickly might jump-start what few brain cells he had left.

"The police never released that detail. They held that back in case there was a break. How do you know exactly where she was shot?"

"I…I…uh."

"It's because you killed her, Judd."

Judd pointed the gun at her. Anger glistened like sweat off every inch of him. She could feel it, smell the rage on him. "She promised me that ring. Said it was as good as mine."

"Chrissy, you should leave," Mrs. Abernathy said. "Leave here now, and don't ever return to him."

Like a deer in headlights, Chrissy looked just as confused as she always did, running a second or two behind everyone else. Judd pointed the gun at Chrissy. "You're not going anywhere."

Chrissy cried and held up her hands in surrender. "Judd, please. You promised we weren't gonna hurt her. You promised it would be easy."

"I believe this is between you and me, Judd. Let the girl go, and I will give you the ring."

Judd looked at Mrs. Abernathy and then nodded for Chrissy to go. "Wait for me outside, and don't you dare do something fucking dumb."

Chrissy grabbed her purse and ran for the front door. At least the girl would have a chance. Whether or not she took it was up to her. The girl opened the door. Outside, rain poured. Through the back window, Mrs. Abernathy could see the sea churn and waves break against the pounding rain.

"The ring, Marilyn," he demanded.

"Yes, okay. The girl has been looking in the wrong place. Help me up and I'll show you," she said. She extended one arm up. Judd didn't budge. "You'll never find it without my help, so either help me up or shoot me." Judd tucked the gun into the back of his pants and scowled. He pulled her up, roughly. She felt her knee crack a little, and her legs started to give. She detested asking for help—especially from him—but there was no other way. "Help me to the desk."

"You try to pull something on me—" he warned.

"And you'll shoot me? Oh please, I'm an old lady. What can I do besides fall?"

He laughed. *High and mighty*. A position he never earned but thought was his, through sheer arrogance and violence. He helped her limp over toward the desk. Mrs. Abernathy braced herself on the desk with one hand and slipped her other hand into her pocket.

"Ring's in the desk?"

"Why did you kill her? Can you at least tell me that?" She stared into Judd's eyes. Evil was the only word that came to mind.

"Easy. I told her to kill you if you didn't give her the ring. She promised me she would, and she broke that promise. She was just like you. Spoiled. Thought the world owed her everything, including chance after chance. Some of us aren't so lucky, and she needed to be reminded of that."

Mrs. Abernathy thought about Alice that night, pointing the gun at her. Begging her mom to give her the ring. Had her daughter really promised this man she would kill her own mother?

If only she could go back in time, Mrs. Abernathy trade her own life for Alice's without question.

Now, she did the only thing she could do well—fall. She let herself drop to the floor, but she didn't brace, instead keeping her hands curled at her stomach. Just like she hoped, Judd moved on instinct, reaching down to lift her up. He hadn't seen the letter opener though. His eyes widened in a dangerous surprise when he felt the brass stab into his gut.

Judd looked down and then smiled. Mrs. Abernathy couldn't understand why at first but then realized the metal sheath was still on. "Dumb bitch." Judd yanked the letter opener, but he only took the cover, leaving the sharp dagger firmly in her hand. He tossed the sheath to its side and reached behind his back for the gun.

She shoved the letter opener into his throat, but it wasn't sharp enough to slice like she thought it would. The sharp brass met the tension in his neck. Muscles and tendons and ligaments. She wasn't sure she had the strength to push it in any farther.

He growled, something low and fierce. Like an animal for the slaughter. Knowing death was imminent. She heard something hard clatter behind him, probably the gun. His hands grasped for the letter opener. He tried to pry her fingers off, yanking on them, desperately trying to pull the letter opener out of his neck.

She thought about Alice. Her exuberant, funny daughter who was great with puns and liked to hum theme songs when she cooked. Then she thought about her daughter in the morgue. Lifeless. Sand-caked. Bloodied.

Mrs. Abernathy wasn't sure where the force came from, but she sat up and, with the movement, shoved the letter opener deep into his neck. She felt something open a little. His windpipe maybe? He gurgled. Spittle and blood trickled from his mouth. There was a hissing sound. Air rushed from the hole in his throat. His hands let go of hers. He collapsed onto his side and then rolled onto his chest, which pushed the letter opener deeper into his neck.

She scrambled out of the way, ignoring the pain in her knee, and watched the man bleed out onto the red oak parquet floors. If he'd just listened to her the first time, he would have known. She didn't have the ring. It was buried with her daughter. Hers forever.

HITCHHIKER

by Barbara DeMarco-Barrett

I killed my boss. Not like he didn't deserve it. Jude, my boss at Kombucha Life, had gone on and on about how it was my fault a batch of kombucha had gone bad, and kept wagging his stinky, acidic finger at me.

I said, "Please get your fucking hand out of my face," but he wouldn't stop, and I snapped. I gave him a little push—a baby push, as far as pushes go—but he slipped on some kombucha on the floor and was knocked off balance.

"What the hell," he said, and hit his head against the stainless steel counter as he fell.

When he didn't get up, I felt for a pulse—there *was* one, thank God, so maybe I hadn't killed him after all—and called 911 from the landline. But I wasn't about to hang around. I would be blamed, and knowing Jude, he'd press charges—the man was sue-happy—and I could *not* get arrested again. I grabbed my backpack and ran out to my Jeep that sat under three scraggly palm trees.

I needed to think, get my brain working right. What just happened? Why me? I could hardly focus on the road.

I needed an alibi. A bunch of drunk people might be the people I needed about now, so I pulled into Knoll's Bar and Grille, a nice little bar not far from the coast with good food and drink. Inside, the lighting was dim. I found an empty high top not far from the stage.

The server, Anna, all smiles, appeared before me. "I recognize *you*!" she said. "It's been a while."

"Too long." I tried to sound as chipper as I could.

I ordered a margarita. Tiny blue lights ringed the stage where the band played "Susie Q." A couple seated at the bar dashed onto the dance floor. He, in a navy baseball cap, green Army shirt, jeans. Not tall, big torso, skinny legs. Heart attack risk, maybe. My dad had that body type as did Uncle Nick, and both died from heart attacks.

She, years younger—though not daughter-young—jeans, tank top, slim, and straight, shiny brown hair. When the song ended, they returned to their stools to slurp from their drinks, and when the band dropped into danceable blues, they returned, at first somewhat tame, but soon he was leading her all over the floor, no room for anybody else. They reminded me of how I used to be a long time ago. Not a care in the world.

The couple sauntered back to the bar and talked, leaning toward each other. Body language said they weren't long married, if married at all. He wore a wedding ring; she wore a band on her middle finger.

Minutes later, Anna set my drink before me and said, "Enjoy!" No darkness behind Anna's eyes. No past written on her beautiful face. I couldn't forget the sound his head made when it hit and how he gurgled a little.

When the band went on break, I finished my drink, paid my tab, and left a 25 percent tip. I worked as a server once and remembered how a great tip could make my day. I wanted to make Anna's day. Same went for the band. I dropped a five in their tip jar on my way out.

The drink had relaxed me, but there was still a shroud of anxiety that grew after I turned the key in the ignition and the Jeep wouldn't start. I would have called AAA, but I let the membership lapse; I could hardly afford my rent with what I made doing kombucha tastings at the farmers' markets. It was the only job I could get, fresh from my stint in jail, because all I did was push her a bit, but the woman called it assault. She stole my parking space but cursed me out for feeling outraged, and like anyone, I got mad.

I took my backpack, locked the Jeep, and walked a few blocks to the signal on Crown Valley Parkway. I stuck out my thumb. I'd take my chances. I couldn't stay here, and there would be no Uber for me. I didn't know who I would call—better that no one else get involved in case this went sideways. And I didn't want to use a credit card; credit cards told everyone where you were. I didn't know where I was going, which didn't help when my bank account was scraping bottom.

A dozen cars passed before one stopped. The unshaven driver looked creepy. It didn't help that he was missing a front tooth. I waved him on, and he called me a bitch. I gave him the finger as he pulled away. I stuck out my thumb again. This time a late-model Audi pulled over. The window went down. I scanned the car for anything that might look awry. It was tidy, no fast-food wrappers everywhere.

He was easy on the eyes: head of curly black hair, trimmed beard, collared shirt over a black tee, husky but fit. Resembled a slightly younger Mickey Haller on *The Lincoln Lawyer*.

"Where you headed?" He had a slight Spanish accent.

"Any place but here."

"I'm headed north," he said. "Los Alamitos Bay Marina."

"What's there?"

"My boat."

Would a serial killer make up going to their boat? He made eye contact. A steady focus. If he was up to no good, I reasoned he would have shifty eyes. Anyway, he should be more afraid of me; I may have killed a man.

"That'd be great. I can carry on from there."

He hit the unlock button. "Come on, then."

I set the backpack on the floor between my feet.

"You never see women hitchhiking anymore," he said. "It's not safe."

"I'm not just any woman." I crossed my eyes and stuck out my tongue.

He laughed. I liked the sound of his laughter, as if he was in on the joke instead of confused by it.

"Why no Uber?" he asked as the Audi took the curves with alacrity.

"Too expensive," I said. "I'm Martine."

"Apollo."

He had the best name of anyone I'd ever met. A Greek god, the god of light. We turned north on Coast Highway. The air smelled salty and damp. On the left stood posh hotels and resorts. The ocean sparkled from the full moon, which I took as a good sign, even though I didn't believe in signs. My mother had believed in them. She said they were everywhere if you opened your eyes and paid attention.

When we hit the Laguna Beach city limits, he said, "You feel like a drink? My treat."

"Why not?" This could also work as an alibi, especially with drunk people whose memories are faulty. If you tell them they saw me, they might agree.

"Do you know the Marine Room?"

"I've been there. Long time ago." I remembered drinking with a red-haired drummer who wore black-rimmed glasses. It was all coming back, though it must have been ten years.

The speed limit decreased to thirty miles an hour. New since I was last here were the yellow flashing lights that span the crosswalks over the highway. About time. Before they installed those lights, you took your life into your hands crossing the street. Great beaches, lousy crosswalks. The lights flashed, and Apollo stopped for a guy wearing trunks, a Hawaiian shirt, and flip-flops, holding a boogie board with a towel around his neck.

We parked on Forest, cut through the post office's parking lot, and walked a block to the Marine Room. In the bar a live band played that old song, "Working in a Coal Mine." How fitting. Kombucha might be a warm and fuzzy, healthful drink, but I've never met an owner of a kombucha factory that didn't pay crap and work you to the bone.

We slid onto stools beside a couple that kept grabbing onto each other so they wouldn't fall, one saying, "Stop tickling me," and the other one saying, "I'm not tickling you; what did you smoke before we left?"

Apollo's phone vibrated. He studied the screen, then set it face down on the bar. His brow wiggled the slightest as he looked over at me. I sensed he didn't want me to ask, which was fine, because I didn't want to know. He wasn't wearing a wedding ring, which didn't mean crap.

The bartender placed a beer before Apollo and a margarita before me. I was ten miles from the kombucha factory. I'd be safe at least for a little while and could drink all I wanted because someone else was driving.

We toasted. The icy concoction was cool on my tongue, tart and tangy.

We watched the band and drank.

Ten minutes later he ordered more drinks for us. My phone dinged with a text from my friend Rosie who did the farmers' markets tastings with me. I turned off the ringer and looked at the text.

Did you hear about Jude? she wrote.

What happened?

He hit his head. He's in the hospital!

You're kidding! Shit. *I've been at Knoll's all afternoon!*

At least my call to 911 had done *something*. Glad I called on a landline, but I wondered if it could lead to me. Did they record those calls? Was my voice glued to a recording in the ether?

Apollo slid his phone into his pocket. "You like boats?"

"I love boats. My dad had a boat. We went out on it a lot. Always from Dana Point."

"I'll give you a tour if you like."

"I like."

Maybe from there I would hitch a ride across the water to Catalina. Get me off the mainland, away from whatever was happening with Jude. It was his own damn fault, all that wagging. People shouldn't wag a finger at anyone, not even a dog.

I knew someone who lived over there, Bebe Bair, though we'd been out of touch. I met her in jail, where she was doing time for embezzlement. If her asshole boss had paid her more, she wouldn't have had to take what was rightfully hers. They call it stealing, but no one can survive in Southern California on minimum wage. Her boss was the evil one, if you ask me.

Back in the car, Apollo tuned the radio to KJZZ. Old school, listening to the radio, listening to jazz. My big brother played in a jazz band; now he was in a prison band in Chino. Try as we might, bad decision-making ran in our family.

I put down my window. He said, "A girl who likes the wind in her hair," and he put his down, too. I didn't like being called a girl, but I didn't mind when he said it. He turned up the radio because a Gary Moore song came on, "Still Got the Blues." He sang along; I swayed in my seat.

North of Seal Beach, we turned off Coast Highway and drove into the marina parking lot. Apollo pulled a duffel bag from the back seat.

"Come see my boat before you take off."

"Sure." In my head, I was planning. I'd find a cheap motel for the night and in the morning come back here when boats were launching and see if anyone would take me to Catalina.

"Help me with something?" He opened the trunk and pulled out two large canvas bags. "Sails," he said. "They're heavy. Think you can manage it?" He handed me one. It weighed a ton, but I was no weakling.

I followed him down a ramp and along a wooden jetty past a dozen boats on either side. Whatever was in the bag didn't feel like a sail.

"What's in this again?"

"I told you, sails." There was an edge to his voice, so I left it alone, but it made me nervous. The bag felt clumpy and hard to balance. I had enough to worry about without worrying what was inside.

I breathed in the night air. It smelled dank and salty, my favorite smell in the world. Reminded me of days on my dad's boat, at sea, adrift. Gulls squawking, occasional boat horn. Wood creaking in the water that sounded like an attic door. Something clanging, soft, as if someone was playing the triangle. The sloshing of boats at their moorings. Soothing sounds.

"Here we are," he said.

He stopped before a 36-foot sailboat. On the back, the name *Pretty in Pink* was painted. Maybe named after that ancient rom-com movie. I didn't even know if he was married. I didn't care. He swung the duffel over the edge of the hull and onto the deck, first his large canvas bag, then mine. I stepped on.

"Be right back." He walked below but left his duffel on deck. On my phone I checked the Mission Viejo police log but found nothing. I texted Rosie.

Hear anything more?

Jude came to. He mentioned a skirmish with an employee. The police asked me about you.

What are they saying about me?

You're the last one he was seen with. They have a description: long black hair, nose ring, tattoos, pretty.

Fuck. I removed the nose ring and dropped it into my shirt pocket.

It was his own fault. He should have mopped up before he screamed at me. After I wrote it, I tried to undeliver it but too late.

Yeah, he's an asshole.

Apollo returned with a bottle of tequila and two shot glasses. "Look what I found," he said.

I put down my phone.

He poured and handed me a glass. "À santé," he said, and we drank.

I walked to the stern and gazed into the water. Was drowning painful? Freezing had to be a more pleasant way to die. You fell asleep as you froze and didn't even notice that you could no longer feel your toes.

Apollo followed. The boat rocked and almost pitched me over the side. He grabbed me and his grip lightened, but he didn't let go and I was glad. We shared a moment.

"Where do you go from here?" I asked.

"I have to get to Catalina."

"I like Catalina."

"Maybe you want to go with me."

"Maybe."

We returned to the deck. He poured us more shots. He was looking at me with this funny, kind of sweet expression, as if he liked what he saw. We sat there like that, the boat rocking, soothing us. He put his arm behind me and rubbed the back of my neck. How'd he know I liked that? I moved closer. We kissed. Tequila makes everything all right.

There was movement in the water and a sort of growling or moaning. A seal's head emerged. Its nose twitched as it sniffed the air, silvery whiskers in the moonlit night.

"I thought seals slept at night." His voice warmed my ear.

"I hear they've been attacking swimmers for no reason," I whispered.

"As long as they don't attack sailors," he said. He moved closer. "Tell me something about you."

"I'm sick of kombucha."

He guffawed. "I wasn't expecting that. Something else."

I shrugged. "Not much to tell. I dropped out of art school to take care of my mom when my dad died. No siblings. I like tequila. I only wear cotton underwear. My favorite artist is Modigliani. Everything in his pictures is long. Long necks. Long trees. You know that painting, *Cypress Trees and a House?* Man, that picture knocks me out. What else you want to know?"

The way he was looking at me, I could tell I amused him. As my dad would say, that's better'n a kick in the ass.

"You're a funny girl." He kissed me again. "Want a tour?"

"Of course."

His hand on the small of my back directed me down the steps to the cabin. The place was so tidy. It was like a tiny house, only tinier, with small round windows on either side. The kitchen reminded me of the Sally Stovetop I had as a kid. Sofa that was more like a window seat. A thin table ran down the center. I peeked into the bathroom. It was no bigger than a restroom on an airplane. A flowery headband hung from a hook near the mirror. He didn't look like the flowery type.

"Now let me show you the boudoir." He nudged me down a minuscule hallway that was really no hallway at all.

With a lame French accent, I said, "Ooh la la."

"Oui, oui," he said, and we fell onto the bunk smaller than a twin bed.

We made out like teenagers. I knew a few guys who could benefit from his kissing instruction, he was that good.

"You smell like lemons." I breathed in his scent.

"I hope you like lemons," he said.

"I love lemons." His hand slid up under my top and down my jeans. The rocking of the boat lulled me, the way I felt on my ex's water bed. My ex had longed for the sixties and seventies, wished he could have been born earlier, how he missed so much. "When you don't know, you don't miss it," I told him.

Apollo's hands were on my arms and back and front, and I thought how good it was that I had hitchhiked and got picked up by him. Then our clothes were off and we went at it. Maybe our coupling was quick—we'd only met—but life was short.

Afterward he lay on his side facing me, running his fingers up and down my torso.

"This morning I never thought I'd be on the boat with a beautiful woman."

"Will wonders never cease." I didn't mean to sound snarky, so I said, "I was thinking the same thing, I mean, about a man," but it was more fun kissing his soft lips than talking, and we went at it again.

"So you will come with me to Catalina?" he said.

"I would love that," I said. "Can we go tonight?"

"Too late."

"First thing in the morning?"

"I don't see why not," he said, which got me going again. Apollo was more than the god of light. He was the god of stamina.

This time we finished and dressed. He went to use the head, and I went back up onto the deck. My phone pinged with a text. *Jude is gonna be in the hospital for a while, if he makes it* is all Rosie said.

I didn't want to know more. I withdrew the SIM card from my phone and dropped it in the water. Bye-bye. I should have done it earlier because I could imagine the cell signals pinging about towers showing exactly where I was and where I was headed.

The morning could not come too soon when we'd leave the Alamitos Bay, and my past, behind.

He was back on the deck, pouring more shots. He slid beside me on the seat.

"What is it with the *Pretty in Pink* name," I said, "and the floral headband? Are you married? Not that I care. That's your business. Curious."

He blew out a stream of tequila-scented air. "I have not been entirely honest with you," he said.

"No time like the present."

"This is not my boat. It's my buddy's boat. Well, not really a buddy. A business associate. He has three boats. He's in Puerto Rico indefinitely. He's opening a resort or something. Something big."

My mind started spinning. I had $160 left in my checking account. I recalled stories Bebe had told me, one about buying a hot car and reselling it, how documents can be faked with a scanner, Photoshop, and a printer. I knew, from my dad, that boat registrations weren't all that different. Bebe might be very interested in this boat. But I wouldn't talk about this with him yet, suggest we sell it, take the cash, and sail somewhere far away.

We were on the deck, he in the captain's chair. I climbed onto his generous lap and straddled him. He played with my hair. I breathed in his lemony-tequila scent.

The night settled in around us, the seals quieted, and the gentle clanging and creaking, and the intense crap I'd been through, made me sleepy. I must've dozed on his lap because he said, "We ought to get some sleep if we're leaving in the morning."

We went below and crashed in the bunk. He hooked up a lee cloth to prevent us from vaulting off the bed if the tide got jumpy.

I slept like a dead woman and woke to the squawk of gulls as the dull morning light squeezed through the windows. I nudged Apollo, who awoke and sweetly said good morning. Beginnings are sublime.

I washed my face, brushed my teeth, and tied on that floral headband to keep the hair out of my face as I made coffee in the dollhouse-sized kitchen. He joined me, trousers, no shirt. He looked good enough to have for breakfast.

We took our coffees onto the deck. The day was gray. Gray everywhere. My least favorite color. It was so foggy I couldn't see the ramp we'd walked down from the parking lot. Mist from the marine layer coated all of the surfaces and the bay. So much for my fantasy of sailing under a blue sky. My dad hated to sail in fog. That meant he had to keep watch for boats and container ships. Apollo suggested we wait till later or tomorrow or the next clear day, but I said, no, we had to go this morning.

"What's the rush?" he said. "We will be together here or there, it does not matter."

Which is when I said, "I haven't been entirely honest with you, either," and told him the story about Jude and about my other two assault convictions in my past, both for self-defense though I was charged. One from a crazy roommate, another from the crazed parking lot lady. And Jude. Jude was why I had to get out of town now. Told him everything. Was it possible to trust someone you met not even twenty-four hours ago? It was, and I did.

He nodded thoughtfully as the damp wind ruffled his dark curls. "I see," he said, staring into the fog. "Then we will go. Let's finish up here. We will get breakfast in Catalina."

I almost said, "I love you," but those were weighted words, so I held back. I'm not *always* impulsive, just most of the time.

We motored from the harbor into the bay. I'd be lying if I said I wasn't nervous, but Apollo said he had it handled, and there was no alternative but to trust him. I needed to leave the mainland *now*. I'd take my chances. I sat on his lap in the captain's chair and borrowed his phone to look up the crime log for my town. There it was, *Assault, female suspect at large*, including yesterday's date and time.

"Bad news?" His forehead wrinkled into a scowl.

I told him.

"Don't worry," he said. "We will be away from here soon. Have you been to Hotel Metropole on the island? We will stay there. It has a fine restaurant as well."

"What would you think about sailing somewhere farther, like out of the country?"

He thought about it. "It is an idea. First I have business in Catalina, then we will see."

At least there was a chance. I said, "I'm starving."

"There are crackers in my duffel."

I jumped off his lap. The boat must have hit a wave straight on because when I reached the floor of the cabin, it knocked me on my ass. I willed my heart to slow the fuck down, withdrew a box of Wheat Thins.

"What was that?" I ate a cracker and offered him the box.

He waved it away. "This is not good," he said. "That cargo ship missed us by a minute. We are like goldfish to whales."

The fog was even thicker out in the ocean than it was in the harbor. I faced forward and bit off the edge of another cracker, but my appetite had vanished.

Things began skittering about the deck, which was when I remembered something my dad always said: *Be sure to prepare the boat. Tie things down.* We hadn't done that at all.

As a jerrican full of water skidded across the deck, Apollo glanced about. "Where are the life jackets? We should be wearing life jackets." He sounded angry.

"That's right!" I said as another wave knocked me down. My dad used to always make us wear them.

The foredeck was in need of dire attention as things on deck were moving about. It reminded me of a busy intersection where traffic signals didn't work and everyone was going for it.

Apollo left the captain's chair to tie things down and lost his balance when another giant wave rammed the boat sideways, and he was flung overboard. I screamed, "Apollo!" and threw a mooring line toward him in the water, but it was too short because the boat was past him now and the waves were taking him in the opposite direction. His arm emerged from the water and went down again. I circled, looking for him, but it was as if the ocean had swallowed him whole. I kept circling and almost ran into another cargo ship. I had to get out of their lane, but back to the mainland or Catalina?

I chose Catalina. Poseidon, the Greek god of water, had taken my god of light. I cried the whole way there, and I'm not a crier. Not ever.

An hour later I arrived at Catalina, where it was sunny and blue sky everywhere. I anchored in Lover's Cove to avoid the expensive mooring field in Avalon Bay, and to avoid notice.

I found an inflatable dinghy and pump below, in a low cabinet beside the engine. I took both up onto the deck and inflated the dinghy. I gathered my backpack, Apollo's duffel, and the crackers and set them on the deck. I wiped down every surface I might have touched and knotted the rag and sheets from the bed and threw them overboard.

I rowed the dinghy to the harbor and walked up the hill where my friend Bebe lived. Muscle memory from a year ago, when I visited.

No one answered the door, so I sat at the picnic table in her backyard, near a trampoline and tricycle. Odd. Bebe didn't have kids. Maybe she had a roommate with kids or had married someone with kids.

I opened Apollo's duffel bag, pulled out the rag used for polishing the surfaces of the boat wherever my fingerprints might be, and walked it over to the trash. I rooted through the duffel. Clothing, toiletries, and his wallet. If there was any way to let a relative of his know he drowned, I would. That was the least I could do.

I found his driver's license in a pile of credit cards, and there was his photo, taken several years earlier, but his name wasn't Apollo. It was Rodrigo Manuel. Below that was another license, same picture but with the name Henry Bautista. And a third license: Ernesto Lopez. Who was this man I had lusted after for less than a day? His registration card for his car was in the pile, but it was for a 2015 Toyota Camry, not a new Audi. A couple of credit cards with his different names. I felt dizzy.

I kept the $1,250 from the wallet, stuffed everything back into the duffel except for his phone—I'd memorized the password when he loaned it to me—and waited on the table beneath the orange tree. My stomach rumbled, and I contemplated walking down the hill into town when the back slider opened, and a woman, trailed by a small child, said, "May I help you?"

"Oh!" I said. "I was waiting for my friend Bebe."

"Bebe no longer lives here," she said briskly, somewhat angrily.

I got up. "Do you know where she went?"

"No idea." The woman folded her arms in front of her as her toddler hid behind her legs. "She owes me big time."

She obviously was not going to invite me in for breakfast.

"Sorry to trouble you. I'll get going."

I picked up the duffel and backpack and felt her eyes on me as I walked around the corner of the house and out to the street. I'd get some breakfast in town and then figure out what was next. All the way down the hill I thought of Apollo/Henry/Rodrigo/Ernesto. There'd be no selling that boat now.

I checked Jude's status using Apollo's phone. *Assault* had become *Murder*.

I texted Rosie. *Anything new?*

Who is this? she said.

Martine!

Whose phone is this?

Borrowed it. Anything new?

They think you're going to Catalina.

Did you tell them?

Of course not!

Fuck! I'd only pushed the asswipe. Was it my fault he slipped on his own damn product?

My heart was trying to escape my rib cage as I slid onto a wooden stool at the bar in Original Jack's Country Kitchen across from the harbor and studied the menu—eggs or pancakes?—when a man sat on the stool beside me.

"Are the sails aboard?" he said.

He was talking to me. "Excuse me?" I said.

"The sails. Are they aboard? You left Long Beach with Henry, showed up here without him. Now you're Henry, or shall we say Henrietta? And you've got some deliveries to make."

"Who are you?"

"Lou. A friend of Henry's." He nodded at the server who set glasses of water before both of us.

"I helped him carry the bags onto the boat. That's all I know."

"Have your breakfast," he said. "Then we have work to do. I'll need the bags."

"You can have your bags and the boat and whatever. I need to eat. I can't remember the last time I had a meal." I could have slept sitting up on the stool. The last couple of days had taken it out of me. I wanted to be rid of the boat, the sails, this guy, though he was nice enough. Maybe someone was sailing to Hawaii, and I could hitch a ride.

We ordered. For me, French toast and tea. For Lou, eggs and black coffee. The door to the outside opened, letting in the smell of salt and the wind on the water. Apollo was out there somewhere. Lou and I chatted about nothing much—the weather, Catalina's backcountry, the films shot there. The server put down plates before us when I heard the sirens. Two police cars pulled up in front. Two cops disappeared around the side of the building, and the other two came inside.

Couldn't they have at least waited till we had eaten our breakfast?

THE SHADOW OF THE TROUGH

by Lindsay Jamieson

Anna says, "You have to tell her, Dave. You can't wait another day." We're just inside the sliding glass doors that lead out onto the deck. She grabs my wrist. She pulls.

"Look. I'll do it," I say. Because that's the truth, but it won't be easy. I should have done it months ago. Every day I wait, I only make it worse. June and I have been married for sixteen years. We met in college. We built TrendX. We work together. We sleep in the same bed… Anna drops my wrist like she can feel my thoughts. What did June feel this morning when I rolled away thinking about Anna? "I will tell her about us," I say. "I'm waiting for the right moment."

"For fuck's sake. There's no such thing as the right moment. We're having a baby in six months."

I yank open the sliding glass door and then the flimsy screen that rattles on its track. Waves roll toward the house with a rhythmic roar no longer muffled by the thick glass. Salty wind blasts my face, and sun, both in the sky and reflected off the water, stings my eyes.

"I get it." I step out onto the deck and into that searing light. A wave attacks the pilings holding up the narrow house, washing away another millimeter of foundation, probably more. Underneath me, the Pacific slaps up at the deck's planks. Another wave hits, dark green in the overhang's shade, and the house shudders. But I'm not worried about erosion now. With my elbows on the hot, weathered rail, I lean out over the churning water.

June and I tried to get pregnant for years. She had three miscarriages; we failed at IVF twice. Which was brutal for her. It was bad for me, too—heartbreaking—but it almost killed June. I told her it was fine, that I was happy without kids. "You're enough," I said. When Anna showed me our positive pregnancy test, my first impulse was to call June. Not to gloat or brag, or to make her feel bad. But there's a baby coming, and for a split second, I imagined June would share my joy; we had tried so hard, for so long. Behind me, Anna slides the glass door shut between us. She always knows when I'm thinking about June.

I stare at the water until my eyes hurt. Because the last emotion June will feel when I tell her the truth is joy. She will be devastated. And when she finds out it's Anna, she'll be enraged. A line of pelicans flies across my view, dipping and rising over the swells. Part of me wishes I were one of them, floating on the wind, worried only about catching my next fish. The leader dives into the water, and I want to dive into the water, too, and swim away. But only for a second. Because, like the bird I'm watching, I now have a family to feed.

It takes my eyes a few minutes to adjust, but as soon as I can see through the glass and into the house, there's Anna sitting with her back to me and the ocean, her long, dark hair twisted up into a clip. I'm in love with her, and we're having a baby. When I forget about June and how I still have to confess, I want to scream the truth about Anna and the baby to the whole world. Why shouldn't I get my happiness? Why must both June and I suffer when I've been given this chance? Anna stands when I return through the glass door.

"I'll tell her this week. I'll find the right time," I say. Anna's wearing joggers and a T-shirt, through which I swear I can see her body transform.

"You do that." She grabs a pile of tote bags, reaches for a baseball cap and her keys. Listening to her jingle while she stalks down the hall to the front door, I love her more than ever. I want to make this right. I text June:

Let's take the sailboat out tomorrow afternoon.

I need to force the issue, and with the scent of Anna's cocoa butter still potent in the house, I have the bravery to text.

There's something I need to discuss.

On the boat, I won't have an out. Anna and the baby deserve this from me. I deserve this from me. I need to purge this dread from my bones and my organs and my skin. June can move on. She's resilient. Always has been. She's much stronger than me.

Okay, she replies, *3 pm meeting with the BOD. I can meet you at the marina at 4:30. Funny, I was planning on asking you to go sailing, too.*

***

"I'm gonna lose my job," Anna says alongside me at the bottom of the metal and glass stairs. "It's not fair. She'll fire me. It's not fair."

"I don't know what will happen, Anna." We're at work, and June is right above us in her office. Can she hear us talking through the floor? "We're going out on the boat."

I knew June had dinner with investors last night, and that if I went to bed early, I wouldn't have to talk. When Anna and I first started, I was so terrified June would catch us that Anna and I only communicated through a Google doc. We've been so careful, no one knows. But still, every time I hear June's car pull into the driveway, every time she enters a room, I fear I've been caught. She'll scream and throw things. She'll cut up and set fire to my clothes. But it's been a year—a year... And she still has no idea. This morning, I found June in the kitchen dressed for tennis and filling her mug with hot coffee. I stood in the doorway, waiting for her to hurl the boiling coffee at my face. She could have grabbed a kitchen knife and stabbed me, but instead she smiled. "I'm looking forward to that sail tonight," she said.

"Me too."

June's only five foot four and maybe 110 pounds wet. So small. I'm always surprised by her size when I see her; she's bigger in my imagination, more imposing, more of a threat. But really, she's a little blond woman whom I've seen cry a thousand tears. The last time IVF failed, she didn't get out of bed for two weeks.

She shrank under the covers. I worried she might not survive. "This hurts too much," she said. "I want to die." But she survived.

"I can resign," I say to Anna at the midpoint of TrendX's first-floor hall. "I'll take my share and go. We can start over somewhere else." John, the intern, runs past, and I swear he throws Anna a look. She's hard not to look at right now with all those hormones shining through her skin. And the cocoa butter smell... Twice a day—three times some days—she rubs it into her belly skin. Standing in a bright rectangle of window sunlight, Anna wipes tears with her manicured fingertips. Walking away is the right thing to do. "We can't take June's company from her."

"It's your company, too. And I've worked here for four years." She's wearing a shapeless dress, but I know what's underneath. "I don't want to give up my whole career."

"Who knows what will happen to TrendX? We might both lose our jobs."

Anna sighs. I can't hug her here. "I just want to be a happy mom," she says. "This is my only chance, Dave. I want to be excited. But all I feel is dread. It's a new life, but it feels like a death. I think the baby can feel it. I do."

"Today, my love. I'm fixing it today."

The row of windows at the top of the hallway wall shows the tops of the palm trees outside. June designed it that way, so it feels like a vacation with those green pom-pom palm fronds cheering all of us on. After today, this will be ruined for June. She hired Anna. Anna was June's fault.

"June," Anna says like *Hurry!* Or *Quick!* Behind her, June's heading toward us down the hall.

"Hi, Anna," June says to Anna's walking-away back.

"Oh, hi, June." She stops but only half turns. "I'm on my way down to HR with these applications." She raises the folder in her hand. It's forced. Anna's losing her touch. There's no point now, really. Soon, she'll be showing. This is the worst thing I've ever done. And what if Anna's right and the baby already feels our anguish instead of our love? My God... Though I've recovered from the other worst things I've done. I cheated on my SATs. That was bad, but it got me into USC. And I forgot all about it. I cheated there, too. I guess I'm a cheater. But I'm not a murderer. I'm not that. I'm not a rapist. I'm not a thief. Not really. I'm an adulterer.

"Are you okay?" June touches my arm like we're still married. We are. We are one hundred percent. Yes, this is the worst thing I've ever done. But then I think about Anna and the baby, and it doesn't feel like a crime, because I'm also thrilled. Adultery is a sin, but I'm not religious. I know it's wrong, but I didn't kill anyone. I made someone. I'm not a murderer. I'm not a thief.

"You look sick," June says.

"Oh," I say. She's right; I'm dizzy and hot and could vomit. I'll run away. I'll take Anna and the baby and run. "No. I'm fine. I drank too much coffee."

"Yeah, that will do it," June says with her hand still on my arm. Like I'm her husband and she's my wife. Her fingerprints press into my skin, driven by hands that are much stronger than they look. I watch her watch Anna disappear, and I think about all the men who kill their wives. I'm better than that. Though when June hears the truth, she might wish I kill her instead.

BY LINDSAY JAMIESON

* * *

I've never been so uncomfortable rigging my boat. The *Trend Setter* was my twelve-year anniversary gift from June. A 38-foot Beneteau I'd coveted for years. The sails were June's idea of linen and silk, which is what you give for twelve years. "I fudged it, a little," June said. And I loved her for it, thought I'd never stop loving her.

If I looked sick in the hall at work, I can't imagine how I look now, pulling the cover off the boat, unlocking the door to the hull. Maybe this isn't the best idea, I think as I descend into the boat's interior. June couldn't give me a child, so she gave me this boat. I check to make sure we have a full tank of gas, the whole time running over what I'm going to say. But while I try to summon contrition, I can't help but imagine a child with me on deck. My child. Anna's child. I always wanted that with June, but it didn't happen. The boat rocks, and I steady myself on the counter in the kitchen stocked with everything you need to cook meals: pots and dishes and knives. We can move to San Diego, maybe. Start over. June can keep the house. There's enough money to go around. Maybe we can all be happy. Maybe it will be okay.

"Dave?" I hear her land on deck.

"I'm inside." My intestines clench, and I'm afraid they might fail. At least June already thinks I'm not well. Maybe she'll take mercy on me. That almost makes me laugh, it's so absurd.

"Hiya," she says while climbing down into the cabin with a stuffed tote in one hand. Her hair is in a ponytail that swings, and she changed from her tailored work clothes into loose white shorts over a black bikini. She's happy, and I'm about to hurt her. But I will do it. We are on this boat, and I will not return to shore until I've finished what I started. I owe that to June and to Anna. And to myself.

"Hi." The bag looks heavy, so I'm not surprised when she heads for the kitchen without stopping first for a kiss.

"I brought dinner," she says while she unloads what look like baguette sandwiches and containers of potato salad, bags of chips. She uncorks a bottle of wine and pours it into two plastic wineglasses. It's the 2015 Qupé Viognier we bought in Santa Barbara. June's favorite. The last time I checked, there was only one bottle left.

"Let's get out there, shall we?" she says, handing me my glass of wine. She knows I have something to tell her. I made that clear in my text. But we have to taxi out of the marina, where everyone hears everything, and where I have to pay attention to the other boats, the narrow channels between the docks. It's not the place for a heated fight. June must sense that the conversation we're about to have requires the privacy of the open seas. She can scream at me in the swells. She can throw things. She can cry.

We fall into our routine. I jump onto the dock; June unties the lines and throws them to me. Once I'm back on board, we motor away from our slip and toward the channel in water that smells of fish guts and gasoline. I steer while June enjoys the ride from the bow.

"Sea lions," she yells, pointing at two pups lounging on a green-carpeted section of dock. One of them barks.

"Cute," I say, and I wish for a second I could go back and undo what I've done. But then I feel like a traitor against Anna and the baby. My child, whom I can't wait to show sea lion pups.

We're past the buoy channel marker now, and there's no turning back. There's no way out of this mess but forward. So, I drive with a purpose, as if I'll reach a destination where this nightmare will cease. As if I can sail my way out of this mess.

Outside the shelter of the marina, salty, wet wind—10 mph SSE—smacks my face and my bare arms, reminding me why I love to sail. Why we live in Malibu. Why June gave me this boat. We reach the open sea, and June helps me raise the sails. We're efficient as always, working together as a team. When both sails are raised and secured, I turn off the motor and let the wind catch hold of the boat. "Thar she blows," June says in a pirate's voice. And, though we've done this hundreds of times, for a moment, we're silenced by our awe.

The boat keels so the starboard side hovers over the water while we speed through the chop and out toward the sinking sun. June returns to the bow and sits cross-legged on the deck, smiling in the warm late-summer rays, while I tack a few times, angling us as far north as possible so we can return on an easy broad reach.

"Let's go way out," June says. "Maybe we'll see a whale."

The sun sits about two inches over the horizon now, so I can't go out more than a couple of miles, or we might not make it back on the wind, which tends to die at dusk. But I know June loves the deep swells. The water looks almost flat from the marina, or from the beach, or from the deck of Anna's rental on the PCH. But when you're in it, it's not flat at all. In some places, the Pacific off the coast here is over a thousand feet deep. The *Trend Setter* becomes insignificant, just a tiny structure easily tossed. Even on a calm day, the swells are so big that during the few seconds the boat's in a trough, we can't see the shore. The water's clearer there, too. Endless aquamarine. And it's warm today. June might even decide to swim. We could both use a spiritual cleanse. If only we could skip the talk. If only I could move on with my life without breaking June's heart.

"I'm hungry, and I want a refill. You?" June shouts to me from the hatch. I don't want to be drunk, but I could use the courage.

"Sure." I notice her toenails are painted black when she jogs into the hull and when she returns with the wine.

"That's the Qupé?" I say, hoping it will spark a starter conversation I can use as a lead-in.

"Yeah," she says. "Why save it, right? Nothing lasts forever."

"No, nothing lasts forever," I say. "June—"

"Hold that thought," she says before heading back inside for the food.

I sip my wine while I trim the sails and set us on a beam reach heading for the horizon, pointing directly into the orange setting sun. She's below, and the rush of the wind and the chop of the waves lull me. I'll read *The Voyage of the Dawn Treader* to my child. *The Odyssey*. A cry from the galley brings me back to the reality I need to face.

"June?" I switch on the boat's autopilot and jump down into the salon. There's blood everywhere, and June's holding a serrated knife.

"I cut my hand," June says, holding the knife—pointing it at me, if I'm honest. "I was trying to cut the sandwiches." They must have rolled off the counter because their insides are now strewn across the cabin; a tomato slice sits an inch from my foot. "I'm sorry about the mess, all the blood," she says. It's a white kitchen, and she's managed to stain the banquette cushions and even the teak floor.

"Careful," I say. A swell hits, and we both stumble toward the sink. I reach for the knife, but she pulls it away. "Can I have that, please?" I say. She looks at the knife and down at the cut, fleshy base of her thumb, still oozing blood. "Give me the knife."

For a second, she stares at me, and I think maybe I don't need to say anything to her at all. She looks at me with that bloody knife in her hand, and I feel like she already knows the truth. My wife can hear through floors and see through walls. She lunges toward me with the knife.

"Hey!" I flinch. But she's just reaching for the tomato slice.

"Here," she says, handing me the knife. She tosses the tomato into the sink, then wraps her hand in a dish towel, stopping the blood.

"What a disaster," she says, looking at the flung-about pieces of sandwich, the bloodstains. "I made a mess of your boat."

"Is it okay?" I ask. "Is it deep? Do we need to go to the ER?"

She presses her hand between her legs, staining her white shorts with blood. And I'm reminded of when she had that first miscarriage. We were at the Draycott, and she was wearing a pastel flowered dress. "What is it?" I asked because she'd been chatting and laughing, but then she winced. She rearranged her skirt and looked down. "I'm bleeding," she said with all the knowledge of what that meant in her voice. She pulled at her skirt. "I'm bleeding," she said, her face drenched in a flash flood of tears.

"No," she says. "No, ER." She opens the banquette bench and fishes out the first aid kit. She finds a Band-Aid and adheres it to her cut.

At first, I think what I'm smelling is blood, but it's not. "I smell gas," I say.

"I have something to tell you, too," she says. "But this was your idea, so you go first."

"Hang on, I'll heave to." I climb on deck ahead of her, my heart beating louder and faster than the chop, and backwind the jib. June emerges wearing just her bikini.

"I didn't want to stain any more of the boat," she says. "It's bad enough as it is."

"It's fine, June," I say, though it is a lot of blood. And there's more. She reclines on the cushioned seat and props up her feet like she's tanning her legs, completely unaware that her blood-soaked Band-Aid is leaving stains like an engraver's mark on the tan upholstery. The whole boat will have to be cleaned. I suppose that's a fair price to pay for what I'm about to do.

"So?" she says.

The boat rises and falls on the deep water. It's hard not to think about everything swimming beneath us while night encroaches. Feeding time. I wonder how many large fish have picked up the smell of June's blood. "I have to tell you something," I say.

"So you said." She stares at the shoreline and the Santa Monica Mountains rising into the dark blue dusk like a humpback.

"I'm having an affair." The words are out, but she doesn't react, so I wonder if she heard me over the ocean noise. "I'm having an affair."

"With Anna," she says. "I know."

And I want to yell at her. "You know? Why—"

"Didn't I tell you, Dave?" she says, now looking right at me. "Are you really about to blame me?" She swats at the loose strands of hair blowing into her face.

She could have confronted me. She could have saved us all this time. I stare at her profile, which has changed over the years. Her nose is longer and beakish; her jawline isn't as sharp. She's so much thinner than in college that I'm not sure I'd know who she was if we hadn't seen each other since and met now. It takes college classmates a few minutes to recognize me, too. Especially since I embraced my bald head. She laughs, and I remember her at eighteen and twenty-five and forty because her laugh was always captivating, and nothing about that has changed.

"Did you see the picture of you drooling over her at the retreat?" she says while reining in her laugh. "It was right there on the TrendX photo-share site. At first, I thought maybe you just had a crush." A seagull lands on the railing beside us and nods like it's watching, waiting for the next big reveal. I want to log into that photo site and see what June's talking about. What picture of me ogling Anna? "But then you started making up bullshit lies," June says, that laugh now long gone. "You're a terrible cheater,

Dave. The worst. That private Google doc is literally the property of TrendX. Everyone knows."

That can't be true. Someone would have said something to me. I would know if our secret was out. If June can read that doc... Why hasn't she killed me by now? The seagull launches and flies into the quickly dropping orange sun. It's getting cold, and I'm shivering. Goosebumps cover June's naked, tanned legs.

"I followed her when she took that day off." June stands and leans into the cockpit. The loose bits of hair around her face fly and dance in the wind. She's been wearing Invisalign, and her teeth are now straight and sharp.

Two months ago, when Anna went to the OB, I met her there for the ultrasound. "You had a league match," I say. June left that morning wearing her team uniform. She had her extra racquet in her bag.

"Was I?"

I should feel shame now; I've been caught. But instead, I'm mad I've been played. "You spied on us?"

"Us?" June says. "Us!" She leans out over the water and squints into the last of the sun. She takes several deep breaths. She closes her eyes.

I unlock the wheel. I need to call a lawyer. I don't know what I thought would happen out here. It's not like there's a possible amicable ending. She's probably got Laura Wasser waiting for me on the dock, with everyone from the office, no doubt, all of them on her side. I want to fucking hit myself. And what's worse is that right now, poor Anna's at work, surrounded by people who know what we've done. I'm better off out here with the literal sharks.

I tell myself that it will be fine. I try to settle my pulse. I got away with the SATs and my plagiarized thesis. If I'm being honest, I've gotten away with plenty more over the years. Who cares if everyone knows? So what if I get fired? Sure, it will suck for Anna. She's sensitive. But California is a no-fault state, so no matter what, half of everything is still mine. And more than anything, Anna and the baby are mine. You can't take them from me, bitch. Go fuck yourself.

I stand to get a better view of the water and the shoreline, which is still far away. The boat traveled too far while I was in the salon tending to June, who, now that I think about it, probably soiled the boat out of spite. She tricked me into thinking about her miscarriages, too, with the bloody white shorts. "Wait," I say while turning the boat toward the marina. "What did you want to tell me?"

"Oh yeah," she says, pulling back from the rail and leaning toward me. "Remember I had you sign a whole stack of papers last week?"

Evelyn brought in a giant folder; I signed for twenty minutes without reading a page.

"New life insurance policy for me," she says. "Suspiciously large."

That night at the Draycott, it took me a minute to understand what "I'm bleeding" meant. It should have been obvious, but the truth is, at first, I wasn't sure. I thought maybe she'd cut herself, but that didn't match the expression on her face. Her smile fell; her eyes retreated into her head. It was like she was extinguished, and for sixty seconds, I didn't know why. I feel like that now. This isn't about life insurance—or spilled gas. I wish I could escape the wind and the chop and the motion of the water so I could think. I've never been more desperate for dry land.

"You know, Dave..." June swings one leg over the rail and straddles the spot where the seagull gawked. "When I saw you coming out of the doctor's appointment together with that photo in your hand."

We stopped to look at the ultrasound. We kissed in the parking lot. I remember it well. The marine layer was thick, and it was chilly for July, so I had my arm around Anna.

"I wanted to run you both over with my car."

I picture June behind the wheel of her BMW. I see Anna and me kissing from June's point of view.

"But then I'd still be alive. Worse, I'd end up in jail. I don't want to risk that, Dave. But that is what I hope happens to you."

The *Trend Setter* rises on a large swell and then slides down into the trough.

"What are you talking about?" I say, desperate to get onto that broad reach. I hear a clunk beneath me in the boat. Then a motor whirring to life. "What the fuck is that?"

"Bilge pump," June says.

We're over a mile and a half from the beach. Why is there water in the boat? What has she done?

"Are you killing us both, June? What the fuck? Why is the bilge pump on?"

"The gas you smelled earlier," she says. "I punctured the tank."

Thank God there's enough wind. The sails fill, and we're headed back, but the mile between me and the shore feels like ten or twenty. Because I have no idea what the fuck June is up to with the gas tank. I need to get out of this ocean alive. I need to get off this boat.

Then she stands on the rail like a masthead. It takes incredible balance and strength to hold still like that while the *Trend Setter* charges through the darkening seas. I watch her with both hatred and awe. "What the fuck, June? You'll fall." I have an urge to push her then. She would be gone, and I could be free. I would get everything.

"Yes," she says. But I wouldn't be free… She made sure of that.

"Don't!" I yell.

We're speeding toward the beach, but it feels like time slows to a stop. "Don't!" But, with a little bounce, June raises her arms over her head and dives gracefully off the boat.

"Jesus! June!" I let go of the wheel, and the boat spins downwind. I run for the life preserver, but it's gone from its hook. "June!" In water shining blood red in the final rays of the setting sun, her white arms slice and pull. "June!"

I can't jump in after her. I can't abandon the boat. Without the motor, there's nothing I can do. I'm downwind of her, and she knows it. Her arms reach and reach and reach, pulling her upwind with each stroke. "I can't get you, June. I can't save you now. Come back!"

She stops and treads as if she heard my last plea. The swells send her up high, then drop her into the black shadow on the other side. The water is over a thousand feet deep here; we're more than a mile from shore. "What have you done?" I cry. "Come back."

"See you in hell," June yells from the top of a swell. The wind sucks me away from her blond head and her goodbye cry. I'm not even sure if I heard her right, or if I imagined the words. She disappears into the dark valley of the next trough.

IMPOSTER SYNDROME

by Joe Clifford

The divorce was both a surprise and inevitable. I'd like to say it hurt more than it did. Twenty years of marriage should've meant more than the (considerable) equity acquired, most of which (including the house) was going to my ex, Wendy. I wasn't left in bad shape (financially). I knew of men who got screwed far worse. And the most prized possessions still remained: our two beautiful daughters, Lydia and Riley, whom I saw two weekends a month. I won't lie and say there was no acrimony. The timing of the divorce coincided with the girls getting their driver's licenses. We'd been a modern family, with Wendy working the traditional day job, providing those little necessities like health insurance, while I stayed home and "played artist." Her words, not mine. But as a painter, writer, and musician, I also didn't have to be in an office every day, which allowed me to drop the girls off at school and pick them up, bring them to dance classes when they were little, to various doctor appointments as they got older. When I was no longer needed, I was let go, an unskilled laborer replaced by machines that could do the job cheaper.

Still, the end was a mercy killing. I don't recall the moment Wendy and I fell out of love, only that we did. The last five years, we were more roommates than spouses. Separate vacations, beds, trading off hours on weekends to secure time alone. (It wasn't the girls we were trying to get away from.)

None of this alarmed me. I knew several couples who'd been married as long. It wasn't uncommon for spouses to spend time apart. Takes murder out of the equation, I suppose. (That's a joke.) Physically, I wasn't as sexually attracted to her as I'd once been, though Wendy remained fit and attractive for her age. I'm sure she felt the same. Affection waned, sex turned nonexistent, but it's not like we fought all the time either. From my point of view, we ran a family conglomerate with Wendy and me as joint CEOs. The company was successful. Wendy and I still made time for "date nights," a stipulation heavily encouraged by the couples therapist Wendy insisted we see, a dried-out, silver-haired Earth Mother in an oversized muumuu who *never* took my side.

The short of it: While I was under the illusion we were still working on things, Wendy was getting fucked after yoga sessions on Saturdays. (Now I understood the "personal time.")

When I found out, I didn't make a scene. I also didn't try to win her back.

She filed. I signed.

I secured a cozy apartment on the comfy beaches of Pacifica. A bungalow. Perched on soft sands surrounded by dwarf blue chalk sticks and ice plants, it landed a long way from the hills of San Francisco. Over the years, we'd accumulated so much stuff. I didn't want any of it. Let her keep the big house and assorted doodads. I was digging my new place, a minimalist return to roots.

Before meeting Wendy at SF State, I lived on the beach in Santa Cruz. I was swimming by age two, boogie boarding by the time I was nine. While most boys were playing soccer or in Little League, I was surfing. For me, the water offered a spiritual experience. My mother (God rest her soul) used to call me her little fishy. And even if I am now on the other side of fifty, it's hard not to smile when I think about that.

Some—particularly my wife's dopey friends—mocked my return to surfing. To them, I was a sad, divorced dad mired in a clichéd midlife crisis. What did I care what anyone else thought? Especially those adult children Wendy tramped around with. (San Francisco is filled with these types who stay childless, Peter Pan rejects on synthetic drugs. Go to any Renaissance faire or Burning Man. You'll find the oversexed pixies playing dress-up in the dirt.) I was finally *me* again. I knew who I was. I'd lost that for a while. Worse than lost—I'd *given* it away.

I can't tell you the joy—the sheer, unadulterated joy—of that first overcast, cold, and damp morning. Sun yet up (not that light could penetrate the perpetual murk of Pacifica), wetsuit slapped on, I stepped out back, board under arm, and walked across that shaky wooden walkway. Trudging through wet sand, I didn't have to go thirty feet before I was back in the water. It jolted me awake. More than the frigid temperatures, the moment generated an electric shock, like the heavens had defibrillated my broken heart, bringing me back to life.

Paddling out, I waited for the swell, timed my mount, riding wave after wave.

I felt young again.

I felt alive.

Then I got out of the water.

And that's when things...turned strange.

* * *

The beach is no longer empty. Families—mothers, fathers, sons, daughters—spread across the sands, as if this were Hawaii or even SoCal, any place where the weather and water aren't so hostile and unwelcoming. Sun buried behind cloud, I hadn't seen a soul the entire time I was surfing—and I must've been out there for hours. There are signs all over the beach cautioning against swimming. The water here is, at best, contaminated. To even contemplate doing what I've just done, I've needed a skintight rubber suit, doubtfully dissuading the bacteria and industrial waste. I'm a divorced dad in his fifties. I'm less risk adverse. Some of the parents are bringing *their kids* into this water. Then I force myself to remember none of this is my problem. I'm not even a primary caregiver for my *own* children. I've been cast out of Eden, banished to the flats—it's time to worry about what makes *me* happy.

Once I power down the judgmental radar, I can selfishly admit I've never felt better.

Surfing—like playing golf or being an unabashed oenophile—is easily jeered. The culture has been appropriated into heist movies saturated with ham-handed Buddhist philosophy. (Which contrasts nicely against that other stereotype, the Greek God with a golden head full of rocks.) Hollywood hasn't gotten it *entirely* wrong. There *is* a Zen-like component. I'm not talking pithy quotes on the tags of tea bags or filling posh moms' Insta feeds. Surfing produces peace, a sense of being; lost in deep, dark waters, you are separated from the self. Ego sloughs. How can one feel anything but insignificant in an ocean filled with so much uncertainty?

* * *

Today is Friday, which means I get the girls for the weekend. After a nice, long, hot shower and latte at the corner Starbucks, I hop on the 1 and head up 280. Crossing into the city, I ascend steep city streets, pulling up to the large home that used to be mine.

While I'm not looking forward to seeing my ex, I don't hate her. I don't...anything...her. When I am in a relationship, I give everything, am all in, one hundred percent. When I am gone, I take back my heart. She will get nothing.

Wendy and I make small talk in the kitchen. I hear one of my girls yell, "Hi, Daddy." I can't tell which one. Their bedroom is upstairs and far away.

My ex starts complaining about the latest drama at her job, and I couldn't care less. Caring is no longer part of my job description. I know there are many who are fine with this whole "we shared a bed, but now we don't, but everything is still cool." I'm not one of them.

I stare past her shoulder, wait till her mouth stops moving, and then mutter "mm-hmm" or "wow" to not be rude.

My mind drifts elsewhere. I'm thinking of what the girls and I will do this weekend. When they were little, Lydia and Riley loved the Monterey aquarium, but I'm guessing they are too old for petting stingrays. Even before the divorce, the family unit had broken down, the girls bearing the brunt. They've grown older. I know them less.

I hear voices and footsteps in the stairwell. They float lighter, more carefree. It hasn't been long since I saw my girls, but the time away, my morning in the sea—it makes them sound different.

I've started making for the door, my back to the scene. I don't enjoy being in this house. Too many reminders. Even when things end badly, the place you lived was still a home. When that's stripped away, you're the odd man out, a thing that doesn't belong.

It's not until I've cracked the front door open and turned around that I actually *look* at my daughters.

And these two girls are not them.

I don't mean they've grown or changed or I'm viewing life from a new, different perspective. These two girls are *not* my children. They bear a vague resemblance. The one meant to be Riley, I'm guessing, because of the darker, longer hair, is almost passable if I were catching her at a glance and not looking her dead-on. The one who is supposed to be Lydia? Less convincing.

Like a recast in a low-budget sequel, the kind that skips theatrical release and goes straight to video, back when that was a thing.

I haven't said a word. I'm sure my poker face is failing. What kind of joke is this?

I look to Wendy, who, though capable of being unkind, would *never* play such a trick. Never mind the woman has no discernable sense of humor. These imposters' gazes fix on me. Their stares feel like an accusation, inviting a retort. Not sure what I'm supposed to say.

I'm not a deadbeat dad returning from globe-trotting, some hippie troubadour slash absentee parent breezing into town when it's convenient. I've been very present in their lives. In fact, of the two of us, I've spent considerably more time with my girls. Wendy had the day job. I worked from home, even if that occasionally took me on the road.

"You okay, Dad?" one of the girls—the one that's *supposed* to be Lydia, my eldest—asks. She's dressed like Lydia, same scruffy, neo-punk rock suburban style, rebellion softened around harsher edges, anarchy commercialized. Ripped jeans, obscure band tee stretched out at the neck, jangling bracelets, the bleached, shorn, glue-head hair. She's rail thin like my Lydia—both girls are on the slender side—but this version appears stretched out.

"Dad?" the fake Riley says.

What am I to do? This is not some elaborate prank. No one snickers under their breath. Our family doesn't share that sort of humor.

These are not my children.

The moment drags out interminably long. Comically so. And I know the expression on my face betrays an imbecile—you can only smile and bob and mumble for so long. I have no other option than to go along with the ruse. I've been presented with two irrefutable yet contradictory truths: One, these are not my children, and, two, I'm the only one who can see that.

Though I don't *want* to, I leave the house with the two girls, who still answer to Riley and Lydia. Walking to the car, the imposters talk like sisters, laugh like sisters—they address me like my daughters would. There is that vernacular kids today use. Low-key and an over- or misuse of the word *literally*. If I weren't aware of the situation—or I were, say, in another room and overhearing snippets of dialogue, I *might* be fooled. That is not the case.

In my car, I check the rearview, stare intently into the eyes of two teenage girls now giggling and conversing in their own little world. I take these strangers to lunch—they pick a restaurant, Firefly, an eatery both my real children love. Over salads and wraps, the performance continues. They use the same cadence, reference the same relations and relatives—they know *our* life— trips we've taken, inside jokes. Same size, shape, model—but they are not the genuine article. I pay the bill.

I shift into autopilot for the rest of the weekend. At the movies, at Putt-Putt golf, while window-shopping, over breakfast, and at assorted cafés, I maintain the illusion. When I drop them off late Sunday night, I've played a convincing role of Dad.

My psychiatrist, Dr. Goldberg, isn't available on weekends— he made that *very* clear when I started seeing him. How could I explain over voicemail what I'm experiencing? "Hey, Doc. I think my children have been swapped out by body snatchers. Call me back."

I drive to the ocean. It's too late to surf, but I need to feel *someplace* where I belong.

Watch the black waters swell, rise, crest, crash, roll. Walk out into the murky unknown. Let the depths swallow you whole, Jonah to the whale. Become one with nothing.

I lied. This divorce has been hard on me. But it hasn't driven me to the brink of madness. I have not contemplated suicide or anything that dramatic. I didn't go out and buy a motorcycle or start banging a twenty-five-year-old coed who spells her name with an abundance of *y*'s instead of an *i*. I rented a sensible two-bedroom apartment and returned to a hobby from my youth. I am not falling apart, but I can't pretend I am steady.

First thing Monday morning, I drive to my shrink. Under a tree that dips too low, I am here an hour before Dr. Goldberg opens for business. Morning dew and sap splatter my hood. I don't have an appointment. The June sun shines bright if not warmly. The cold breaches steel, slithering through cracks in the metal. I can hear it bend between bursts of wind. I didn't sleep last night. I sat on the beach all night, huddled in a hoodie, watching the early-morning fog crawl across wet sand, certain I would disappear if I left my post.

I check my appearance in the mirror. Eyes sag. Big, black bags. It hits me how little I have. Not materialwise. I'm doing fine in that department. It's family.

I have none.

My mother long dead, I never knew a father. The few friends I had drifted out of my life, to the point calling them now would be shocking. I'd need to explain who I was. And right now, I'm not so sure.

Time ebbs, slowed, inextricably prolonged. I study the clock on the dash. At one point, hand on Bible, I swear the minutes go *backward*. I haven't smoked a cigarette in fifteen years. I see an open market up the block and am seriously contemplating what those cancer sticks cost these days when Dr. Goldberg steers in. Before he can park, I'm out of my car, all but running to the old man.

Dr. Goldberg startles when he sees me, unruly gray eyebrows understandably furrowed.

As I watch him glimpse at his watch, I pray my urgency prompts what comes next.

"I have fifteen minutes before my first session," he says.

His office door has yet to close before I'm unloading. Imposters. Strangers. Doppelgängers. Not my children! I don't worry whether Dr. Goldberg might 5150 my crazy ass. It wouldn't be the first time I needed time away.

To my surprise, Dr. Goldberg simply says, "Prosopagnosia."

I wait for more, because surely one word can't explain this.

"It's a condition," Dr. Goldberg continues matter-of-factly. "Rare but not unheard of. Those suffering can't recognize the faces of loved ones. We don't know the root cause. But like many psychological conditions in this life, stress can play a factor."

The doctor reiterates my past year. The infidelity and divorce. Losing the house. Being forced to move out of the home *I* chose.

And I'm not immune to that other, third stressor: career change. No, I haven't been fired—I don't have a job where I can be—but I've been forced to accept that I bet everything—on my art, on myself—and I lost. If my art sold better, maybe I'd have more confidence, would've felt less desperate, been a better parent, more present partner. Instead of feeling like a loser, which no matter how much I try to fight, I most certainly do. At my age, I don't have any marketable skills, and I'm too tired to learn. I worked so hard to live outside of societal conventions that it's grown too late for me to come back to the fold.

"We will address this," Dr. Goldberg says, checking his scheduling blotter. "I had a cancellation for later this afternoon. Five o'clock. Sound good?"

I nod, unconvincingly.

"I understand how scary this is," he says. "Feel free to read up about it." He laughs, more cough than guffaw. A chortle. "Though rare, prosopagnosia is treatable." He smiles, a kindly grandfather. "Take comfort in knowing you are not alone."

* * *

When I leave the doctor's, the sun has gone away, and it feels like for good this time. San Francisco summers are notorious for their cold and fog. Usually you get at least a *few* hours of sunshine. This deviation leaves me feeling disquieted, unsettled.

I decide that the only thing that might improve my mood is surfing. I race home to get my board. When I get to the beach, it can't be later than ten thirty, eleven.

It's empty. Completely barren. I scan up and down the shore, to the steps leading to the parking lot. Nothing. No people. No cars.

Last Friday morning, before I got the girls, the beach had been crawling with people. Now it's near midday, and not a soul.

The cold fog feels thicker. It drapes over me. I look at the frigid water and search for the strength I used to have. I can't fathom stepping into that icy black pool. I know if I can catch a wave, ride a swell or two, I can get out of my head. I *know* it'll make me feel better. But I can't make myself do it. I am convinced if I put a foot in that sea, I will drown, sucked to the bottom of an inescapable abyss.

Hours on the internet, I search prosopagnosia cases, but it does little to soothe. Personal testimonials only stamp the irrefutable and terrifying. I bear all the hallmarks of the cognitive disorder, a slippery slope to early onset of dementia, which is what took out my mom early, and it wasn't early enough—the last few years, driving hours to a nursing home, only to have her stare at me blankly, with no clue who I was. Is this what I have to look forward to? An inability to recognize the faces of those closest to me? Having to rely on auditory clues? The girls *sounded* like Lydia and Riley. I wasn't totally in the dark. I'm also a long way from the light.

My house feels like a prison cell. Periodic, random noises rattle beyond these walls, which makes me dart to the window. No one is ever there. I'm not expecting company. Still I see *no one*, *nothing* on the beach. It feels like the world is ending.

When I can't take another minute alone, I drive back north, prepared to sit outside Dr. Goldberg's office until it's time for our appointment, because I can't think of where else to go. I'm not on the highway long before other cars join me, and a wave of relief washes over me. The world is not ending. This isn't the apocalypse. As ridiculous as that sounds, the possibility wasn't off the table.

I have been a patient of Dr. Goldberg for many years. I've driven, bicycled—even walked—from Noe Valley to his office in the Mission many times. Furthermore, I've lived in the San Francisco Bay Area nearly all my life. While street names *can* change, the streets themselves don't. Inexplicably, I find myself lost. I turned up Cesar Chavez, like I was supposed to, and I took a right on Harrison (at least I think I did), but now...I am lost.

The fog continues to grow thicker. The Mexican motifs and rolling carts selling chili and mango, the hood rats slinging on corners tell me I'm still in the Mission District. In my haste to leave Pacifica, I left behind my phone, which is disconcerting enough. I can't map a route. There are no signs; the corners remain nameless. I keep driving, steering on instinct. I don't remember crossing train tracks or going under any bridges, yet somehow I find myself in Hunter's Point, which lands a long way from where I want to be, and I can't, for the life of me, understand why.

This is not a great part of town. I see a familiar site that comforts, a 7-Eleven store. The fog drenches, claustrophobic. A group of kids huddle by the entrance, smoking and drinking. A little voice tells me I am overreacting. I do my best to silence it.

These kids come from a different world. That doesn't make them violent or bad. I walk like I belong.

I don't make it five feet before the pack descends upon me.

"You lost, motherfucker?"

I turn toward the young men—boys, really. None of them can be older than sixteen, seventeen. They're on bicycles.

"You eyeballing me?"

It's surreal how fast my worst fears are manifesting. That's what this feels like: as if *I* am creating an alternate reality. I've conjured a movie scene in my head based on prejudice and hysteria, and now my broken psyche is projecting the action, forcing it to play out.

I try to smile.

The first fist catches me flush in the eye, blinding me, and then I'm in a heap on the ground, four, five boys shouting at me, kicking me. I can feel their rage over nothing I've done. No one comes to my rescue.

Somehow, I manage to separate myself from the scrum and scramble back to my car. I feel shaken and discombobulated. My ears are ringing. I push the engine on and tear out of the parking lot. Back on the road, I look in the mirror, and my right eye is cut. Blood dribbles out my nose. All in all, I don't look too bad in light of the thrashing I just took. I covered my head as well as I could, but my arms and legs, flanks and gut ache. My muscles burn. Tomorrow, I will be covered in blacks and blues. For now I'm thankful my face made it out relatively unscathed. I ought to go to the police, file a report, press charges. I don't.

It's almost time for my appointment with Dr. Goldberg.

I don't drive there either.

Instead, I drive to Wendy's and the house that used to be mine. I need a semblance of order restored. As I navigate murky city streets, steering into my old neighborhood, I feel anything but calmed. Trees in wire pots teeter precariously. Stoops appear crooked, doors slanted.

"What are you doing here?" Wendy asks.

I point to my face, but that elicits no reaction.

Finally, I say, "I was attacked." Still, she says nothing. I wait before adding, "I was mugged."

"When?"

"Just now. Outside the 7-Eleven." I don't tell her which neighborhood.

My ex-wife's eyes rove over me. "I don't see a mark."

"I'm not lying. I was just attacked. A group of thugs beat the hell out of me."

"I didn't say you were lying. I don't see any cuts or injury. I guess you were lucky?" With this last comment, she shrugs.

"Dad?"

I turn up the hall, unsure which of the imposters I am going to see.

Except I don't.

It's Riley. *My* Riley.

And behind her is Lydia. *My Lydia.*

I start laughing. I know this makes me comes across even more unhinged. I don't care. My children are back. Instinctively, I wave them over and wrap them all in a huge hug. It's an unexpected display of affection. Whatever was wrong with me, this prosopagnosia, it was only a brief ripple in the water, a smudge in time. It wasn't real. Everything is back as it should.

I apologize to Wendy for the intrusion, which is rich, seeing as how she was the one who was unfaithful, but in this moment I'm so happy—so unabashedly happy. I thought for sure I was fast-tracked toward madness.

I ask if it would be okay to clean up in the bathroom.

Wendy says of course.

The girls say they'll see me in a couple weeks.

I step into the bathroom and close the door, exhaling, relieved, order restored.

Until I catch my reflection in the mirror.

The man who stares back is not me. He is wearing different clothes. I had on a light jacket over a sweater and jeans. This clown is dressed in a windbreaker and neon elastic pants fat people wear to feel better about the lack of a waistline. I stare at this stranger, this man I have never seen before. Different face shape, heavier jowls, less hair. Worse than the imposter Riley or Lydia, the recast looks *nothing* like me. The reflection that stares back bears a vague *sense* of what *could* have been, something in the eyes, perhaps. A different life path. But his eyes are *not* mine. This porker couldn't paddle out in the ocean. Fat bastard would sink like a stone. His hygiene stinks. Whoever he is, this joker has given up, let himself go. He doesn't even try to maintain appearances.

He isn't an imposter.

He's something far worse.

He's a goddamn liar.

YOU MUST REMEMBER THIS

by Gary Phillips

Three architects were responsible for the design of the Los Angeles City Hall. The Art Deco tower-shaped building with its pyramid roof was inspired by the Mausoleum at Halicarnassus in Turkey, one of the Seven Wonders of the Ancient World. And to symbolize that this, the tallest building in the city, was more than just a municipal fixture, the concrete used to construct the edifice was formed via sand taken from California's fifty-eight counties, and the water from each of its twenty-one missions.

Today was a blustery day as the man in the blue serge suit took the stairs from the twenty-sixth floor, where painted portraits of the city's past mayors and various functions were held. He then went through a door onto the observation deck. There were two others outside taking in the view, a man and woman. She had on a large brimmed hat and had to keep a hand to it to prevent her chapeau from blowing away.

"What a view," she enthused.

"Yeah, you can see the oil wells up there in those hills," the man said, pointing.

For some reason the woman found that romantic as she turned to him, and tilting her head upward, they kissed. It was like an image out of a motion picture, her with her hand on her hat and him with an arm around her slim waist. They separated, becoming aware for the first time of the third person on the deck. He stood apart at a corner, leaning on the rail as if taking in the view as well.

Self-conscious, the two held hands, and the couple left the deck. The other man remained where he was for a few more moments, looking out upon the city and its environs. A biplane flew overhead toward Mines Field the airport, Hubert Morrows noted absently. He pulled a pack of Chesterfields from his jacket's inner pocket and, cupping his hand to the wind, lit a cigarette. He took a few puffs, the smoke streaming away from his face in a westerly direction. He flicked the cigarette into the air, watching it twist and turn on the invisible currents of wind as it was blown to who knew where. Morrows then removed his shoes, the tiles of the deck warm through his socks with penguins on them.

Muttering, "There is no other way," he climbed onto the railing atop the sternum-high wall and briefly balanced there in his stockinged feet, appreciating the breathtaking view, took a swan dive off of city hall. On the ground a man eating a hot dog purchased from a cart vendor threw up as Hubert Morrows violently impacted the concrete steps, his head exploding in brains and bone and blood, splattering the surroundings.

The following day, in newspapers such as the *Los Angeles Examiner* and the *L.A. Times*, variations of their headlines recorded that Hubert Morrows, forty-eight, the city controller, had committed suicide by jumping off of city hall. One reporter speculated he'd removed his shoes so as to not scuff them and to be buried in them. The police were investigating, but already the rumor of embezzlement was being bandied about unofficially and was the talk of patrons in saloons along Spring Street. Buried in the back pages of those papers was another article about a death. This had to do with the body of a colored domestic—what she was called—being found in an alley near the intersection of Thirty-Ninth Street and Central Avenue. Her throat had been cut.

In the two largest Black newsweeklies, the *Sentinel* and the *California Eagle*, the housekeeper's murder was on the front page. The dead woman's name was Estelle Parmington. Her mother, Unida Parmington, carried a folded-over copy of the *Sentinel* with her when she went to see Nelly Marsh in her second-floor office in a three-story building not too far south from city hall and not too far north from the Stem—the hub of the Black belt of businesses, cafés, and clubs in and around Central Avenue.

"You've got to help me, Miss Marsh, you just have to." The mother sniffed and dabbed at her wet eyes and nose with her handkerchief. She sat in her mourning clothes in the plain wood chair before the equally plain walnut desk. There were only a few items framed on the walls of the humble office, including the private investigator license issued by the State of California to the woman sitting behind the desk in a swivel chair. There was also a lone, battered filing cabinet and a coat rack with a slouch hat and unadorned, black, knee-length coat on it. When she'd first entered, this struck the mother as an office lacking a feminine touch, particularly given the attractiveness of its occupant.

"The police aren't going to do anything. The detective who finally talked to me asked who Estelle was seeing. He said it looked to him like some boyfriend of hers lost his head probably because she was giving it away to some other fella. Where they found her body he figured she'd been in one of them jazz clubs and got all liquored up and dancing loose." She looked off, choking up. "He almost snickered in my face he was so tickled at what he was imagining, you hear what I'm saying?" She teared up again.

The tan-hued, black-haired woman on the other side of the desk reached across to pat the older woman's hand. "I understand what you're saying, Mrs. Parmington. I know about the police in this town." Marsh wore an ornamental, rough-hewn, silver ring set with a Marsh diamond.

"Yes, well, of course you would. How they treat our people," she said, shaking her head.

"What particulars can you give me about your daughter, Mrs. Parmington?"

The grieving mother gave her a brief rundown of her daughter's past as well as the address to her daughter's apartment and a key she possessed.

"Was she working currently?" Marsh asked.

The mother frowned. "She was. It was some kind of combination home and office, the way I understand it."

"You know where and for whom?"

"That's the funny thing. Usually Estelle was pretty talkative about where she was working and the sort of people she encountered in these businesses. She was mum on this employer."

Marsh was making a note on the steno pad she'd opened on the desk. "You have an idea why?"

"I can't really say..."

Marsh regarded her, an inquisitive look composing her face. "I'm not the police, Mrs. Parmington. I won't laugh at you."

The mother smiled. "I had the feeling she was sort of embarrassed about the job. She was making top dollar, I know because she'd recently bought a few things for her place she needed, like a new toaster. But she was never forthcoming about the man, about what he did, you see."

Marsh underlined her note about this. "Not to endorse the behavior of the detective, but do you think there's anything to Estelle being in one of the clubs the night before her body was found?" A milkman on his route had seen her feet sticking out in the alley on his early-morning rounds. As he was Black, he'd been quoted in the *Eagle* but not the white press. The private eye had already read the article on the murder before she'd gotten the call from Mrs. Parmington. Marsh ran a small boxed advert in the *Sentinel* as well as the *Herald Examiner*. The three-line listing read: TROUBLE? NELLY MARSH INVESTIGATIONS AXminster 7-9987.

"My Estelle had her head on straight, Miss Marsh. Sure she went out to have a swell time now and then, what young woman wouldn't? Look at you. But she weren't no runaround gal, no, she was raised better than that." The mother leaned forward. "If'n there was some guy giving her grief, she would have told me. We were that kind of mother and daughter." She tapped the desk with her finger as she talked.

Marsh said, "Yes, ma'am."

Mrs. Parmington crossed her legs at the ankles, stealing a glance at her purse, then back to the private detective. "About your rate."

Marsh said, "Let me see what I can find first, then we can figure that out later. You see to a proper burial for Estelle."

"Bless you, Miss Marsh, bless you."

Not too much later at the deceased woman's apartment on a shady street on the eastside, Marsh momentarily stood in the doorway after unlocking the door. The windows were closed, and she noticed the faint smells of mothballs and dime-store perfume. An ironing board was still set up with a cold iron on it, and a box of starch rested nearby. She stepped farther in and quietly closed the door. She began to look around, and as she did so, Marsh had the impression she wasn't the first one to do this in the apartment. There was mail on a side table. Quickly shuffling through them, she could tell from the postmarks the older envelopes were on top, indicating they'd been previously handled. That could mean nothing, but in the kitchen, two of the drawers had not been closed all the way. She tested them and found they slid open easily. Marsh was certain now someone other than Estelle had been here, and it hadn't been the cops, as they wouldn't have been that neat.

Conducting her own search, Marsh found no notation or indication of who had been Estelle Parmington's employer. From what her mother told her, she'd answered an ad in the newspaper, but that had been at least two months ago, and Marsh wasn't inclined to go back through a set of archives and run down a mess of help wanted ads. She did, though, find a note on the calendar with a picture of a Champion spark plug on it. It was in a woman's handwriting about a hair appointment with Lucille this Thursday at the Bronze Allure Salon. In the phone book she found the address for the beauty parlor, which was on Vermont. She drove over there in her Hudson Terraplane.

Inside the shop she asked the owner, an older woman hunched over a romance pulp at the front counter, for Lucille. The woman, arched eyebrows and an immaculate finger wave hairstyle, smiled sweetly at her visitor. "She's right back there," she said, turning her head slightly, then returning to her reading.

Marsh stepped past, and a good-sized but sturdily built, copper-skinned woman came up to her after seeing to one of her customers under a hair dryer. She gave Marsh a clinical once-over as she wiped her hands on a small towel.

"Hair like you got, honey, with that Creole blood of yours, I can give you a cut like Myrna Loy. Make all them fellas at Jack's Basket lose their minds when you stroll in."

"I'll consider that. I'm trying to find out some information on Estelle Parmington."

Lucille's face went gray. "Shame, what happened to her. She was real nice people."

"Her mother hired me to look into her murder."

Lucille got animated again. "What, you some kind of private eye like on one of them radio shows? Girl, they call you LA Blackie?" She laughed, touching Marsh's arm.

Marsh chuckled with her. "I've been called a few names. You have any idea who Estelle worked for? I'm trying to put together her last hours before, well, what happened to her."

Lucille shook her head. "No, sorry, I can't recall who she said she might be cleaning for these days. She did say there wasn't much cooking involved. Seems this guy was what they call a vegetarian."

"She must have said something about her work, gossiping about the conditions, the demands, the usual, right?" Marsh said.

Lucille looked over Marsh's shoulder. "Sorry, but I've got to get back to my work. I sure hope you can help her mama out." She turned and went back toward the rear of the shop. Marsh considered bracing the woman but knew better than make a scene. Doubtless her co-workers and the customers would rally around her, and that would get the private eye nowhere.

Reluctantly Marsh left the shop and walked to her car a few doors down. Two white men leaned on her coupe, both of them smoking like they were on break. One wore a straw boater, and the other was in rolled-up shirtsleeves and suspenders. Marsh realized they must have been on watch at Estelle Parmington's apartment and had followed her over here. Maybe they'd been bird-dogging the mother from the get-go, she considered. They both straightened up as she got closer.

"How you doing today, chickie?" The one in suspenders let his cigarette drop to the sidewalk, but he didn't grind it out. "Nice day to be out in the park feeding the pigeons, ain't it?"

"Blow it out your ear," Marsh said.

He looked at his partner. "Hear that? The mouth on these dames these days."

"Yeah, ever since they got the vote," straw boater replied. He thrust a finger in her face. "Now you keep your pretty nose out of that colored gal get'in her 'less you want the same, you savvy?"

"Oh, please, I'm just a poor woman doing what I can to make ends meet." Marsh had teared up, holding her purse up toward her face as if to ward off further harsh words. "I'm only trying to keep the water on, okay?"

Suspenders sneered at the other one. "Just like a frail, folding when the going gets tough."

"What should I tell Mrs. Parmington?" She sniffed and opened the pocketbook, seemingly searching for her handkerchief.

"Tell her you looked into it and you didn't find nothing," straw boater said, turning away.

"How about I tell her the case is heating up."

"Huh?" Straw boater turned back around, and Marsh brained him with the butt of her .38 revolver, tearing the hat's mesh. He stumbled forward, crashing into her, throwing her off balance. His ruined hat came off his head and fluttered into the gutter.

As this happened, suspenders had an opening and rushed forward, punching Marsh in the face as she tried to right herself. But she still had her gun and, not too dazed, shot the hood in the foot.

"Aw hell," he blared.

Marsh was wrangling with the hatless one who grabbed her by the shoulders and shoved her against her car. He held her gun hand in his large fingers.

"I'm going to teach you good, twist," he growled. "You won't be so damn good-looking when I'm done with you."

"And I'm going to teach you better manners." She kneed him in his privates, and he gasped, his grip loosening. She got out of his grasp, stumbling backward.

"Hey, what y'all doing to that lady?" came a shout from a grocer who'd stepped out from behind his stalls.

"I'm calling the police," came another voice from above. A woman in hair rollers leaned out of her upstairs window, shaking a finger. "You gray boys can't just come around here manhandling us."

Straw boater was looking up at her but addressed his wounded partner, "Let's get out of here."

"What about my foot?"

"Hop."

And he did just that with help from the other man as they hurried off and got into a Chevy and roared away.

"Hey, honey, you okay?" It was Lucille from the beauty salon. She picked up Marsh's purse and handed it to her. She leaned in close. "Look, I didn't say anything 'cause Dee Dee, the owner, she don't want no trouble with the cops. But you come around to the Norbo about six, okay?"

"I sure will."

At fifteen after six, in the bar of the Norbo Hotel, Marsh bought Lucille Farnes a gin fizz. It was one of the places in town outside of the Black belt that catered to a mixed clientele.

"Here's how," Marsh said, clinking her Greyhound against Farnes's glass.

They each had a sip, and then in answer to Marsh's question, the hairdresser said, "Can't say that I really know much more about what Estelle was up to. Fact of the matter she was kinda hush-hush like she was worried."

"Worried her boss would retaliate against her? Like spilling secrets?"

"Yeah, something like that." Farnes had more of her drink. "What she told me when I was doing a touch-up for her about three weeks ago was she had the feeling this guy—she called him the Professor, was using his abilities she said to some shady ends."

"Was she any more specific?"

Farnes shook her head. "No, but I had the feeling this Professor was some kind of soothsayer and had all types of well-to-do clients. He saw them mostly in the evening, and she worked days, but I guess she must have overheard this or that at some point, and it got her thinking cap twirling, as my granny would say."

"She say a name? Usually these crystal ball types like to put on the dog with a mystical-sounding title for the suckers."

"She did not. I do know he's downtown, but that's all I know."

"That's helpful."

Drinking more Farnes said, "So, Nelly, just where are your folks from?"

Marsh laughed and signaled for refills for the both of them.

The following evening, an aging janitor with a big belly and a handlebar mustache checked his pocket watch and, setting aside his push broom, took the stairs down to the first floor and waited by a side door. At the prearranged time there came a knock, and he opened the door a crack to the visage of Nelly Marsh.

"As always, a pleasure to see the enterprising sentinel of justice," he said in his accented English. Fritz Banner had been born in Salzburg, Austria, in 1888 and had fought for his country in World War I. At various times in his life since then, he'd been an ambulance driver, a fireman, owner of a mortuary, and a manager of a nightclub in Paris. These days he was part owner in a gambling ship called the *Venture* three miles out from the Santa Monica Pier. The ship was once owned by the late kingpin Charlie Crawford, who was gunned down several years ago in 1931. Banner also owned a cleaning service while also maintaining the front of being a humble janitor himself. His crew had contracts cleaning several municipal buildings where he could access records and other pertinent information as needed. Few knew of his dual identities. Marsh, though, was one of them.

She stepped inside, holding a small, white box tied with a string around it. "I brought the apricot strudel from Zingerman's." She waved the box under his nose, and he inhaled.

"Wunderbar," he enthused.

At a small table in the break room, the two ate the strudel and drank freshly brewed coffee from paper cups. He'd placed a thin file folder on the table as well.

"That's the information from the license plate you memorized, liebchen."

"Thank you."

The old man pursed his lips. "This fellow, Horace Matthews, who owns that Chevrolet, I've heard of him. He is not what one would call a model citizen. I know, for instance, he has a couple of markers around town and beat the last man who was sent to collect with a sap, putting him in the hospital."

"Who of us are model citizens, Fritz?"

"You should exercise caution."

"Don't I always?"

He forked in more of the dessert. "Back in the war there were soldiers who were so scared they peed their britches." He had more strudel. "Others were wound tight like a watch spring ready to unleash. Others still had a sort of anticipation on their face. Bullets whizzing by, shells exploding in front of them, yet they'd stare out from the trench, rifle at the ready, just waiting for the commander to yell 'charge' so as to vault onto the battlefield and engage the enemy."

He paused, moving a bit of the pastry around on his plate. "It is that eagerness I sometimes see in that arresting face of yours."

"I'll be careful, Mother."

"I can lend you one of my…associates if you wish."

"He would cramp my style."

"Still I worry."

She leaned across and gave him a peck on the cheek. "Maybe it's Matthews who should be worried when I put the vamp on him." She batted her eyes for effect.

"But's he's seen you already."

"To quote Houdini, 'What the eyes see and the ears hear, the mind believes.'"

Banner stared at her quizzically.

* * *

The curvy blonde in the low-cut dress put a dark Russian cigarette between crimson lips. Two men from opposite directions hastened to light the cigarette for her.

"Thanks, boys," she said, pulling her head back and jetting a stream of smoke toward the ceiling.

"How about a Manhattan, doll?" one of the men said.

"Sure, why not?"

The other guy drifted away. The illegal casino was in a red-bricked building accessed by the gamblers through the Hi-Top Bowl, a bowling alley in Culver City. At this time of night the patrons would go to a metal door on one side of the front of the building. There was a sliding eye slot in the door, installed in the days of Prohibition. Like back then, you gave the password and were let in to follow a short hallway to another door marked *Storage*. In that room, which actually contained boxes and the like, another guard sitting on a stool operated a hidden switch and opened a disguised door in the wall, letting you into the action. Fritz Banner had told Marsh there were hidden peepholes in the casino for spotting cheaters and rowdy drunks.

"What do they call you, lovely lady?" The man had curly black hair, a bend in the bridge of his nose, and crow's feet beginning at the edges of his eyes.

"Lola."

"Yeah, yeah, that suits you swell," he said.

"What's yours?"

"Sol," he said, his eyes on her chest.

As they made small talk, the disguised Nelly Marsh kept an eye on Horace Matthews, who was at the craps table. He wore a crisp, new straw boater pushed back on his head.

"Fade line is right, eights the point," announced the croupier.

Matthews rolled the dice. The cubes banked off the apron, and the point was made. "That's what I'm talking about," he said, scooping up the dice.

Marsh said, "Excuse me a second, would you, Sol? I have to powder my nose." Marsh got off the bar stool and headed into the women's restroom. She passed a pleasant-looking, medium-built man in owlish glasses and a bow tie. He looked to be a department store manager, but Marsh knew from Banner he was the owner of the joint. He called himself Anton Rolf, but that was believed to be an alias.

Alone in the bathroom, Marsh took a moment to freshen her lipstick and check her disguise in the mirror. Aside from the blond wig, she'd used an actor's putty to change the shape of her nose and make her face fuller, less accent on her cheekbones as they were more prominent naturally. She'd also put a Southern lilt in her voice.

"No time like the present," she muttered at her reflection, and stepped back out into the din of gamblers trying their luck. Sol was at the bar, waiting her return. Not wanting him to try and put the arm on her later making a scene, she went back over to him.

"So, Sol, honey chile," she began as she sat next to him. "I like a drink as much as the next girl, but seems to me we should get down to brass tacks."

"What are you getting at?" he eagerly responded.

Marsh lowered her voice, smiling seductively. "How about you and I blow this pop stand and find us a nice, quiet room somewhere?"

"Oh yeah," Sol said excitedly. "I knew tonight was my night at the cards, but this, wow!"

"For thirty dollars plus the room rate." Marsh put a hardness in her voice.

"Wait, what are you saying?"

"I'm saying a girl has to eat, Sol," she said matter-of-factly. "You got the cash, then we play house for a little while and have a good time. But that's it, when it's over, it's over. We then go our separate ways." She made sure to regard him with as much affection as a snake does a mouse it's about to dine on.

"Look, how about I buy you a burger and we talk, get to know one another?"

"How about you buy me a pony? Jeez, grow up, will ya?" She got up and, downing her drink, stalked off. Sol gaping after her. It could have gone the other way, Marsh considered, but she knew the going rate working girls were charging these days, and had purposely asked for a higher price. Even if Sol was inclined to pay for a roll in the hay, Marsh had noted the inexpensive coat he wore and the calluses on his hands. At workingman's wages, thirty was asking a lot.

Marsh stood back as Matthews rolled the dice. He lost at times, but on balance, his arm was hot tonight. Men and women were gathered around the table, urging him on. Believers in the gambler's notion that if good will were bestowed on one of them, surely some of that would spill their way. Too, they were making money on the fade.

"I can't be stopped tonight." He rolled again. He didn't make his point, but he didn't crap out. Bets were made for and against him as he plucked the dice from the green felt.

"Maybe this will help." Marsh as Lola had inserted herself between Matthews and a portly man who kept yelling, "Way to go," each time Matthews won, patting him on the back as well.

She pulled the hoodlum's fist with the dice toward her lips and blew on his hand.

Matthews's face lit up like a boy getting that bike he wanted on Christmas.

If he recognized her, he didn't let on, she observed. He turned and rolled.

"Damn," he shouted when he made his point. He turned back to her, a hand gripping her upper arm. "Don't you go nowhere, sister." Booze was evident on his breath.

She'd lowered her head so as to look up into him with bedroom eyes. "I'm not going anywhere, shugah."

He grinned broadly, resuming the game. For another fifteen minutes, he remained hot, but then after three busts in a row, it was clear he was cooling off. "My mama didn't raise no fool, I know when to quit while I'm ahead." Matthews picked up his cash and handed the dice off to the next player—the portly man accepted them as if it were Excalibur pulled from the stone.

Matthews flapped the bills in his hand at Marsh. "Why don't you and I celebrate?"

"You read my mind, big boy."

"You're new around here."

"Just got to town." She gave him her false name, and he his real one.

"You an actresses?" They were walking toward the bar, her arm in his.

"Why yes," she said in a bubbly voice. "I'm hoping to get a screen test over at MGM." The studio was less than two miles away in town.

"Seems I might have seen you some where before." He frowned, trying to dredge up the memory. They were near the bar. Fortunately, Sol was busy at one of the poker tables.

"Get me a drink, will ya? I'm a bit parched. A Manhattan, please."

"Of course." He got the bartender's attention and ordered the drinks. Matthews came back to her.

"Could be you've seen me in a movie," she began, wanting to address his question to divert suspicion. "I've had small parts in a couple of films. You know, usually the one who faints at the sight of the body, or as the cigarette girl."

"Sure, sure that must be it."

Their drinks came, and she made sure to slowly sip hers. Matthews was ramped up, raring to go. They chitchatted more about the movies as Matthews downed his bourbon.

Marsh said, "Shall we go someplace a little quieter? Get to know each other without this buzzing around us?"

"I know just the place. It's a sweet little bar over on Motor."

"Then let's motor over there." She tittered.

"Yes indeed."

Walking out, they passed a man leaning against the outside wall. He was glassy-eyed, clearly drunk. Matthews put his hand around her shoulders, and she didn't shrug free. "My jalopy's right over here." He pointed at his car as they walked. There were a few light poles providing weak circles of illumination across the parking lot, interspersed with pools of darkness.

When they got in the car, she put a hand on his knee as he tossed his hat onto the back seat. "What kind of work do you do, Horace?"

He was staring at her face. "I fix things, baby. I got what you could call a select list of big-timers I work for." He cocked his head.

Marsh squeezed the knee, batting her eyes like she'd shown Banner and sounding breathless. "That sounds so exciting."

He thumbed his chest. "I'm an exciting guy, Lola." He moved to kiss her but stopped when he felt the muzzle of a gun pressed against him. He moved back. "Hey, what's this, what's your play?"

Marsh had taken his gun from his shoulder holster. "Who the hell is the Professor?"

"What are you getting at?"

Apparently he still hadn't recognized her, Marsh concluded, though he'd sobered up due to the surprise. "That's not for you to worry about. Answer the question." She jabbed him with the gun.

He snapped his fingers. "Wait, you and that other dame must be partners, that it?"

"Something like that. Now about the Professor."

"I'll tell you this for free. You best keep that cute little nose of yours out of his business."

"Hey, stop neckin' in there, this here's a family gambling joint." The drunk had slammed his hands on the side of the driver's side window, pressing his face to the glass.

Momentarily distracted, Matthews came at Marsh.

"You kids play rough," the drunk said, somehow not registering the gun the two grappled over. He weaved away into the dark.

Forced back against the passenger's door, Marsh's body pressed down on the latch, and the door came open. She tumbled out of the car, Matthews's gun out of her grasp. She got up, seeing him dip down to the car's floorboards looking for the rod. She ran, having had the foresight to wear chunky heels just in case. The Chevy's engine roared to life, and Matthews plowed toward her. He'd found the gun and stuck it out the window. Sobered up, he didn't shoot given he was still a distance from her , knowing it would bring the guards. His hesitation allowed a running March to get behind a parked car. The Chevy sped up, clipping the bumper of an already dented Buick.

Marsh kept moving and gained one of the dark areas on the lot and ducked down behind a row of cars. She could hear Matthews creep along in his car in low gear. She stopped to listen. The sound of the Chevy's motor receded, and she chanced to take a look over the hood of one of the parked cars. She didn't see Matthews. Marsh got up and ran as fast as she could, hoping to make it to her car. She rounded a parked DeSalvo, and headlights came on. She was fully on display in those lights. The Chevy leaped forward, bearing down on her. Marsh again dove, this time onto the hood of a Mercury. Matthews went past, his brakes squealing as he stomped on the pedal. The Chevy bucked sideways. Matthews ground the clutch, trying to get it in reverse. But he let the clutch out too quickly. The engine stuttered and stalled.

Crouching down as Matthews gunned the Chevy to life, Marsh ran toward the rear of the car. Given the part she was playing, she hadn't brought her gun in the small clutch bag she'd used for the outfit. But no fool, Marsh had strapped her granddaddy's straight razor to her thigh. She ripped the side of her tight skirt to get to it. Flicking the razor open, she slashed the back tire. Off she ran again as the Chevy turned around. Bent over, she got busy at another car's tires. As Matthews once more zeroed in on her, running on the flat, Marsh whirled around, hurling and like an Olympian discus thrower, hurled two hubcaps at the oncoming car. The hubcaps struck the windshield, Matthews instinctively turning the wheel to avoid them.

Marsh was in his headlights, a wall behind her with a painted advertisement for Helms Bakery bread on it.

He yelled, "I'm going to fix you good, you nosy broad."

The car was almost on her when Marsh dropped and rolled out of the way. Matthews hit the brakes. The tires' rubber having already been stripped off the rim, the vehicle skidded more than he intended, sparks flying out from underneath the screeching metal. The Chevy crashed into the wall. Matthews's head went through the windshield, glass everywhere. Steam rose from the front of the vehicle, water dripping to the ground from the cracked radiator. Marsh had to put the blond wig back on as she ran to the car and got the driver's door open. Given the general noise inside the casino, she hedged that no one had heard the commotion. That didn't mean she should be lollygagging either. She ducked inside the car. Matthews was alive, groaning, blood dribbling from numerous lacerations in his head. She started going through his pockets.

A man smoking a cigar stepped outside and saw the wreck. He sauntered over to get a better look. "Hey, what's going on there?" He stopped several feet away, not quite sure what he was seeing. A woman flashing a lot of thigh was bent inside the car; had she been the driver? Did her dress get ripped in the crash? He also wondered.

"Miss, you need help?"

Having turned up nothing of use on Matthews, Marsh was now digging through the glove box. In there were several brochures advertising something called the Houses of the Seven Stages of Enlightenment. She took one and, backing out of the car, aimed Matthews's gun at the curious civilian.

"No, beat it," she said, waving the roscoe. Blond hair partially covered one side of her face.

"Whatever you say, lady." He backed up and ran off.

Marsh used a handkerchief to wipe down surfaces she'd touched in the car's interior. She got into her car, and as she backed out, one of the bouncers came out for a smoke break. His mouth gaped at the sight of the smashed-up Chevy. He ran toward it, and Marsh drove off in the opposite direction.

Later the cigar smoker's description to the cops of the mysterious blonde would include his observations that "She must spend time at the beach. She had a great tan. And easy on the eyes, if you know what I mean," he'd added.

* * *

Barney Hilliard studied his handiwork in the mirror, turning his face to the left, then to the right. There, he rubbed a finger on an area he'd missed. He turned on the faucet and wetted the spot and applied a bit more lather. Two passes with his safety razor eliminated the errant whiskers under his jaw. He splashed warm water from the basin on his face to rinse it clean. He dabbed his face dry and then put face cream between his hands and rubbed them on his face, working the substance into his pores. Thereafter he used his custom blend of makeup to hide the wrinkles around his eyes, and a judicious application of kohl to give them the hint of an almond shape. He rechecked his dye job of his sandy-brown hair going gray at the temples—gray he took efforts to hide. He combed and brushed his hair. Appearance was part of what he was selling as Professor Konis Manku, possibly of German and Chinese origins, educated in renowned European universities. A much better story than a farm boy from Racine, Wisconsin, which he actually was. He splashed on his special blend of cologne and rolled down his sleeves and inserted his jade cuff links in the shape of an ankh. Tie and coat on, Hilliard as Manku checked himself out one more time, then exited his bedroom on the second floor of the rented Victorian mansion in Bunker Hill.

Descending the stairs, he called out, "Roy, are you here?"

Roy Seaton in suspenders came through the kitchen swing door, munching on a sandwich. He hobbled some, given his foot was bandaged underneath his sock from Nelly Marsh having shot off his little toe. But he was getting used to his new sense of balance.

"What else have you learned about this troublesome woman?"

"Not much," Seaton admitted. "She's got that office, a gun, and one hell of a right cross."

"She hasn't been back there since the incident with Horace?"

"Not a peep."

Once Hilliard learned what had happened two nights ago at the casino, he'd told Seaton to keep watch on Nelly Marsh's office. She hadn't returned to it, and there was no other listing for her in the phone book.

"You think maybe the mother might know where to find her?"

"I sincerely doubt such. That young woman strikes me as someone who knows how to move between the lines." The same could be said for him, he realized, grifter, spiritualist, psychic, now healer employing techniques learned in the "Far East." His most successful con yet.

"What's that mean?" Seaton asked.

"It means we better keep an eye out for her as she will turn up again. Maybe in disguise like she did with Horace." He was certain the leggy blonde had been the private eye. He also considered she might show up here wearing a new face as well. But tonight was his usual client, a matron of some means from South Pasadena.

Checking his watch, he said, "Okay, make yourself scarce. I must prepare the parlor."

Seaton grinned. "Whatever you say, swami."

"Now, now"—Hilliard wagged a finger, also smiling—"you must believe."

"In the almighty dollar." Seaton returned to the kitchen.

That evening, the fraudulent professor did a consultation, as he called them, for the well-off woman whose name was Selma Westmore. She was a good-sized woman who wore several necklaces of gold and silver and several rings of the same metals. The parlor contained tasteful furniture and rugs, along with plaster reproductions on the walls, and shelves of masks and symbols of various mystical persuasions as befitting one of Manku's supposed background. Fragrant incense burned in a thurible suspended on chrome chains from the ceiling. They sat at a round table sans crystal ball.

"I have the utmost confidence this affliction will clear up, dear lady," he said, regarding her recent episode of gout. This after prognosticating if she would meet another man as dynamic as her late husband. And that she should she go on the weekend outing with friends to Lone Pine for her internal balance. "I have the proper medicines to alleviate your pain and worry."

"You are magnificent, Professor Manku, simply magnificent."

"I do what I can, gentle one, I do what I can."

The stuff he gave her were tablets that did curtail uric acid buildup along with several placebos. Some twenty-plus years of being at this hustle, Hilliard had learned quite a bit about human anatomy. He had to. The chumps wouldn't come back if they didn't see results.

"Now please," he began, having returned from the kitchen with a kettle of hot water and teacup and saucer. "You must drink the Elixir of Eminence to truly benefit from this most blessed encounter."

"I feel so invigorated after each of our sessions, Professor."

"As you should, as the fates allow." Hilliard knew a lot about drugs, having been a user of morphine and cocaine. In his experimentations he'd stumbled upon a formula for a hypnotic mix. The more doses he gave his clients, the more he bent their will to his. He poured the tea and handed the cup and saucer to her. She drank it down as they talked more; then he refilled her cup and she had more. About halfway finished with the second round, her eyes got glassy, and her speech slowed down as she stared straight ahead.

"Let me take that for you," Hilliard said, removing the cup from her hand, which was suspended near her mouth. He gently pushed her hand into her lap. Hilliard sat back, folding one leg over the other. "Have you been to the bank as we discussed last time?"

"Of course I have, good sir," she answered. "I have set aside the sum we discussed, ten thousand for the orphans."

"Yes, the poor deserving orphans," he said bemusedly. "Did you happen to bring the check with you, dear one?"

"Yes, certainly." Still staring straight ahead, she reached down for her purse at her feet and opened it. She removed a check and placed it face up on the table. The check was made out to an Idic Enterprises.

"Wonderful, dear one, simply wonderful," Hilliard said, clasping his hands together. He stood and she did too. "Now as you know, the elixir can drain you before it surges back to recharge you. Roy will drive you home in your car." His man liked driving the big cars of the swells he bilked. The widow drove a doozy of a Duesenberg, he'd said.

* * *

Nelly Marsh took the camera lens away from the window. There had been a slight gap between the curtains, and it gave her a view of the charlatan and his mark in the parlor. The photos alone wouldn't convict him, but that's not what she was out to do. Considering her tough upbringing, Marsh didn't have much in the way of sympathy if some man or woman rolling in dough got took. That was unfortunate, but she was out to do what her client had asked her to do. Easing out from the shrubbery, she was careful not to make a noise. She was in dark clothes, trousers, and a black satin shirt.

"Hey, how you doing?" Seaton stepped in front of her, his .45 aimed at her eyes. "I'll take that." He reached for the camera.

Marsh attempted to brain him with it, but the thug was quick. Motivated as he was to pay her back for blasting off his toe. Like she'd clubbed Matthews outside the beauty salon, he thonked her with the butt of his gun, twice on the top of her head. She wilted to the ground.

* * *

"Good thing I was on my way to warm up the old lady's car," Marsh heard as she came to.

"And obtained her camera."

Marsh came fully awake. Her head was pounding. She was in the parlor and shackled to one of the fine Victorian chairs in there.

"Ah, our guest is now with us," Hilliard said in his cultured Professor Manku voice. He stepped closer to her, hands in his pockets. "You are quite the pest, aren't you?"

"And you're quite the huckster."

He bowed slightly. "I'll take that as the compliment you intended."

"You're a caution," Seaton said. "Want me to cancel her ticket?"

Hilliard gestured with his hand. "Let's not be hasty with this one. She's special, I can feel it."

Seaton side-eyed Marsh, a nasty grin on his face as he looked at his boss. "Gonna give her a taste of the elixir?"

"Yes, I think that would be superb. In fact I think a double dose is called for." Hilliard stepped out of the parlor.

Seaton bent toward her. "You in for a treat, girlie."

"Which one of you killed Estelle?"

"Why you care so much for that dead colored gal?" He frowned, crooking his head to one side. "Say, maybe…yeah, you're mixed, ain't you? Got some jungle blood in you, or is it Mex?"

Marsh glared at him. Hilliard returned. Not with a tea set this time but a hypodermic.

"Undo her sleeve, Roy," he said.

Seaton did as ordered.

Marsh gritted her teeth as the needle was inserted into her vein and the concoction was pumped into her. A sense of euphoria consumed her, and she felt elated, floating along and open to possibilities.

"She going under," Seaton observed.

Hilliard said, "Yes, but she has a strong sense of self. But I'll be able to mold her as I want."

"Yeah you will," his underling quipped.

Hilliard lowered the lights and turned on music involving an organ and a theremin, an electrical instrument that made out-of-this-world sounds through oscillating frequencies. The overall effect was pulsing and probing, a hypnotic melody that carried his words into her, breaking down his prisoner's resistance.

"Can you not feel it, Miss Marsh, the invisible cosmic waves that surround us, yet we go about our daily lives unaware and not tuned in. Well I am here to tune you in, to see to it that you receive that which you are entitled to."

"Yes," she answered, staring straight ahead.

"Good, good," he said, his upper body swaying with the music. "You must rid yourself of your inhibitions. You are a butterfly who must free themselves from the chrysalis that has nourished you but is now constraining you. Struggle, see in your mind how you must be free. And in freedom you will be unstoppable, indestructible. Is that not so?"

"Yes, it is so."

"You got her, boss," Seaton whispered.

Hilliard pressed a finger to his lips, then continued. "Come and fulfill your destiny, Nelly Marsh. Fly now and show the world how free you are, how magnificent is your ascendency over all the insignificant trials and troubles of this mortal veil. Your first step in the process is for you to walk out this door and into the traffic at the corner. Mere traffic signals mean nothing to you, Queen Butterfly. Come and show us you are above fear and above the constraints of lowly mortal law."

"I will," she said, vacant eyed.

Hilliard signaled for Seaton to unshackle her.

"Rise and be all that you can be," Hilliard said.

Marsh rose slowly, staring off into the near distance.

"Go forth and meet your fate." The charlatan waved a hand at the front door.

Marsh started to walk, passing by the small table where the widow had sat. The tea kettle was still there. She snatched it up in a blur and, spinning around, swiped it across Seaton's face as he leaped at her, knocking him back. She reiterated the blow, and this time he fell to the floor, his head bloody. She took his gun and put it on a stunned Hilliard.

"How did you shrug off the narcotic?"

She showed him her hand palm up. There was blood on her thumb and at the base of one of her fingers. "I turned my ring around and dug the diamond and rough edges into my skin. It was enough pain to cut through the fog of your brain dope." The ring was a gift from Helena Dyton, who owned a jewelry store on the block where her office was. Helena's husband was in jail for murder and stealing from that store. Facts the private eye uncovered.

Marsh stepped closer to Hilliard, poking him in the stomach with the gun. "Now let's get some answers, shall we?"

He didn't like the look on her face.

* * *

It was quiet along the hallway in General Hospital as the nurse's rubber-soled shoes squeaked across the polished floor. She was prim and proper in her uniform and cap, her auburn hair pinned atop her head. She stopped at a particular room, putting her ear to the door, listening. This time of the morning, a few minutes past two a.m., the patients were asleep. She opened the door and stepped inside quickly. It was gloomy in here, but one of the patients in this shared room had left the light on over their bed. She slipped past the slumbering man to stand alongside the bed of a snoring Horace Matthews, who lay on his back. The soft brown-eyed nurse watched his chest rise and fall, rise and fall.

When Nelly Marsh got the drop on Hilliard and his muscle, she'd made the supposed professor give the hood, Seaton, a double dose of his elixir to loosen his tongue. She tied and gagged Hilliard and questioned Seaton. From him she learned it was Matthews who'd slit Estelle Parmington's throat and his idea to dump her in the Central Avenue section. Estelle had inadvertently overheard something she shouldn't have. The suicide of the city controller was due to him realizing he'd embezzled funds at the behest of being hypnotized by Hilliard and his drug. Hilliard had been discussing this with his men, and the house cleaner had been finishing up a longer day than usual. Matthews knew how the police would concoct a certain scenario of her death and do nothing about "just another shine killing."

Marsh inserted the drug in his vein and whispered in his ear, finishing with "You must remember this." Thereafter she helped get him dressed and got him out of there unbothered. She dropped him off in front of the LAPD's central headquarters on Main Street.

He went inside to confess and turn over the murder weapon, a switchblade with his prints on it. Both the white and Black papers carried stories about the lurid goings-on at the House of the Seven Stages of Enlightenment.

HEART OF A WHALE

by Daniel Pyne

Down coast in Long Beach, where the Watchorn Basin inlet high tide ripples, liquid slate, smoke glowers in low-rent thunderheads from a new Palos Verde brush fire. The lazy water glimmers its reflection. Distant sirens keen. Streetlights blink on even before the soft-boiled sun has set.

Civilian sonar analyst Allison Dekker sits safely at the helm of her basement station inside Fort Arthur, a Naval outpost so long ago decommissioned that few people know it exists, but still home to a semi-clandestine and, yes, largely forgotten outpost of Sonar Intelligence.

Tasked with listening for hostile underwater interlopers, Aly has her console speakers rumbling instead with the deep plaintive song cycle of a distant fin whale captured by the array of passive acoustic monitors scattered across the vast wilderness of Pacific Ocean. In a logbook that she keeps on a shelf under her keyboard, screens, and CPUs, she records a date, a time, a location that her GPS algorithm can approximate. Aly knows this whale by sound but double-checks the frequency: fifty-five hertz. Perfect pitch for the key of A. She's been searching for weeks, waiting for its return to the Southern California Bight. A wall map of the world's oceans has a rainbow of pushpins plotting where Fifty-Five's been heard on other Navy hydrophones. Hawaiian archipelago to Point Conception, Baja to the Arctic ice.

Her screens flicker, wane dim, go blank as power fails. Aly curses softly, sits back blind, unsurprised. Flashlights stab the station darkness before the generators kick in to harsh the building's corridors with glaring backup. Protocol dictates no reboot of her equipment. Acoustic analyst Dekker's shift is over, five hours early.

Lit raw by the emergency lights, like a gas-pump island, the nearly empty officers' club bar allows Aly a quiet cocktail before she joins the freeway commuter gridlock. She texts Glenn: *u ok?* No response. Bartender Jared, square-jawed civilian, trim, Black, frightfully handsome, has an Allison crush that he tries to hide. He knows she has a boyfriend, and his undisguised disappointment over it always clouds Jared's sunny smile.

"How's Fifty-Five?"

"Back singing," she says. For some reason, she tells him that a whale has a heart the size of a small car. Jared blinks, looks confused.

Also singing is the acoustic guitar of a musician on a stool in the corner of the bar. "Easy listening jazz, they call it," Jared says. "Trying him out. A budget-bin Ed Sheeran, if you ask me, which nobody does." Aly tries to remember who Ed Sheeran is. "The XO wants to open happy hour to the museum staff and local civilians."

"Not exactly warm and intimate, this light," Aly says.

Jared concedes that it could be better. Maybe he can scrounge up some candles.

Aly takes her adult beverage and settles at a table near the makeshift stage. The guitar player finishes "Here's That Rainy Day" and takes his break. Aly is the only one in the bar who claps.

"Vike," the musician says when he comes back with cola on ice. He sits down as if she's invited him. "Vike Maas. Double-a-s," he adds, chewing ice. "My stage name is Mucho." Aly wonders why.

"Lamely ironic," Vike admits. "Mucho Maas. Because, you know, I'm really not." Pale with pinkish highlights, he looks Danish, if anything. Generic Norseman: Sprout enough beard, he could be Ivar the Boneless on that History Channel show. And in this town, who knows? Maybe he is.

"These fucking fires," he says, a statement that they both understand requires no response. Then he asks, "How'm I doing?" and admits to her that easy listening music isn't really his thing.

"What is?" Aly asks him.

Vike seems stumped and doesn't answer.

Jared is watching them, too intently, Aly thinks. She feels a twinge of rootless guilt but lets it slide. To keep things friendly, she tells Vike Maas her name. No, she's not Navy. Yes, she works for the Navy. Or with them, depending on whom you ask.

She's praying he won't flirt; she's already determined that he's not her type. His leather jacket is unzipped; underneath, a droopy Weezer World Tour tank top screams sleazy but shows off a lean, good body, a little skinny but not at all unattractive. His eyes are sad. He seems lost.

Glancing at her watch, Aly tries to estimate whether, if she leaves soon, she'll have time after braving traffic to make dinner as a surprise for Glenn. Normal shift, she wouldn't be home before midnight. He's usually parked in front of the television with a local small-batch craft beer by eight. There are pork chops defrosting in her fridge, fresh baby asparagus. Maybe some polenta would be good.

Vike makes a strange kind of stream-of-unconscious chitchat, doesn't flirt. He talks like a man who's been shattered and put back together poorly. Parts missing, parts left over. He has a tic; he has an infrequent stutter. Smells faintly of cigarettes. Something bad happened to him in Cuba, he says but doesn't elaborate. "Now there's a lot I can't remember," he admits. Crazed scribbles are inked all over the backs of both hands and up his inner arm.

For a moment, though, his face lights up. After his happy hour gig, he tells her, he's headed to Hollywood for a show at Club Pandemonium. "Mickey Madrid," Vike says. He scored tickets, last minute, by chance. Aly doesn't know rock and roll, but Vike sounds so stoked it's contagious.

"Sounds like fun. You taking someone special?" Aly asks, not really interested, but hoping to help him keep the glow. Truth be told, she's had her fill of damaged men.

Vike only wants to talk about Mickey. "See, I feel like I know him," he confesses to her. "I feel like his music is *my* music." He gestures vaguely, as if spent, his eyes going overcast; he looks lost again. "No clue why, though." After a hesitation, he reminds her, sheepishly, "I have some issues with my memory," then shows her the wilderness of crib-note chords written in blue ink on his hands and arms, in case he loses his way during his gig.

When the next set starts, he dedicates a song to her. She doesn't recognize it, hates that she blushes. Petulant Jared chops limes behind the bar, but no one else is even paying attention. Vike's slender fingers move across the frets like they know their way in spite of him.

Aly's gone before he strums the last chord.

* * *

From the freeway she can see half a dozen rip-like flare-ups from another active burn that limns the Dominguez Hills. To the north, lowriding Santa Monica mountains loom ghostly, shrouded. Huge swaths of the South Bay are blacked out. Street crews clog local roads, working overtime. Breathless all-news radio makes it sound like the whole LA basin is in flames.

A sluggish river of headlights and taillights carries Aly inland. Smoke swirls and eddies through the crawling cars like trench gas. Power is down in her neighborhood. Dead traffic signals and all the resulting mess. Resurgent Santa Anas bend the skinny palms in prayer; the air has an aftertaste, fever hot, and Glenn's car sits in the driveway, dusted in ash.

Home already. She hopes he hasn't eaten.

Her little townhome is spartan, modest, always something of a surprise when she returns to it. A tentative respite for an unsettled soul. Her parents helped her with the mortgage. The monthly payments leave her with scant to spare, but no matter:

She can never decide what furniture to buy, anyway. Or where to hang her posters, so they're still stacked against one wall.

She senses a stranger before she hears Glenn's labored grunting. He's not alone. Something prevents her from turning on lights, announcing that she's home. She tries to convince herself that Glenn is doing his yoga in the spare room, that his best friend, Marlon, is with him, bitching about some promotion he didn't get, but Marlon thinks Glenn's yoga thing is lame, and Marlon doesn't use Chanel nor own the little, soft leather Prada handbag slumped on the kitchen island next to three dewy, jade-green IPO empties.

No, down the hallway, up the stairs, in the bedroom, on Aly's brand-new California queen, her boyfriend is having Olympic freestyle sex with a woman whose face Aly can't see because of the exotic positions. She's surprised how unsurprised she is by this. Glenn tends to harbor a lot of freaky ideas from online porn, and Aly, big-boned and, well, languid in her lovemaking, doesn't favor him any complicated improvisation.

This girl should be a gymnast, Aly thinks. Balance beam. Pommel horse. A Taijitu tattoo curves gently across the woman's ass. Yin and yang.

The pretzeled flesh, the soft-heaving shadows. Syncopated breaths that do not stir her. Aly's out-of-body, watching, for a long time, from the doorway. They don't notice her and she doesn't say anything. Her thinking stalls. After a while, it becomes a strange, almost silent movie; if she hears anything, it's the whale call of Fifty-Five, from memory. Before they finish, she closes the door and backs away.

In the living room darkness, she sits and checks her phone, scrolls through Instagram without really seeing. She listens until her home goes quiet. She feels stupid; she feels free. Her hands are cold. Her heart still beats.

An upstairs door squeaks open, then squicks shut. Stairs creak. A shape separates from the darkness of the hallway. The naked girl from Aly's bed walks, luminous, clutching a bundle of clothes, around the kitchen island, where she roots through the Prada purse. She's gorgeous, maybe twenty-five. Flawless skin, long waist, breasts on the small side, which Aly wishes hers were. There's clean underwear in her little bag, a white thong that Aly watches the girl stretch over narrow, silky hips. What does she eat? Aly wonders. The putative gymnast wriggles into a simple shift that she tugs down over the tattoo and, turning, tossing her hair, sees the other person in the room for the first time.

With dark amber eyes, mostly in shadow, vaguely Asian—or maybe that's just a conceit of her mascara—she studies Aly. But seems not to judge her.

A long, awkward, silent moment stretches between them. The girl's neutral expression tells of neither triumph nor regret. She slips her feet into flip-flops, stuffs a frilly bra and limp black thong in her bag, and leaves the townhouse without looking back or saying anything.

As if Aly weren't there.

A backwash of expensive perfume lingers long after she's gone. Weary fire engine sirens sing, muffled from somewhere far away, like the mournful sonic keening of her whale. The world's on edge. This feels like a pivot. She doesn't wonder how he met her or whether this was the first time. Aly sits, expressionless, trying not to think about what might happen next, for a while longer. She hears a sleepy Glenn call out a name, not hers. She doesn't answer. The living room air seems to shift and settle. Warm light bleeds from the hallway. A shower comes on.

Somehow, Aly finds the strength to walk out.

* * *

A lowering, sooty pall blankets the harbor.

Long Beach skyscrapers cut to size by the fume.

She tastes the Watchorn's familiar sour, salty air.

Main power's still out when Aly returns to Fort Arthur. She doesn't know where else to go. Whatever it is she's feeling, she wants to feel it alone.

Flickering crimson-glass votive candles lend the officers' club a bordello vibe. Jared makes her the new complimentary craft cocktail he's been fussing to perfect. He doesn't ask why she's back. His big hands dance, surprisingly deft and gentle looking. Gin and elderflower and god only knows what else. Aly lies, tells him the drink tastes great.

Jared seems to see through her but accepts the praise with unexpected grace. "Work in progress," he admits. "It's on the house."

The happy hour guitar player, Vike, has long ago finished his gig and gone. But he's left something for Aly. Jared goes in back to find it.

The fin whale she calls Big Fish Fifty-Five is not the only so-called lonely whale that's been discovered and tracked in the Pacific Ocean. There was a big fuss made over the first one, dubbed Fifty-Two. Its unique call frequency led everyone to want to believe it was the last of a dying subspecies of *Balaenoptera physalus*, calling for a mate. Made for a good, sentimental story. Because other fin whales sing in a much lower register, the whale might not be recognized or understood. This spoke to disenfranchisement, isolation, the inability to connect. A metaphor for modern life. Less-romantic explanations involved plastic debris that possibly got lodged in Fifty-Two's blowhole, or a genetic malformation in its air sacs that interfered with normal echolocation.

Conspiracy-minded outliers insisted it was Russians or Chinese intelligence throwing out misdirection and distraction to mask their evil plans. Certain online incels were convinced it was just more evidence of the feminazifying of nature. The persecution of an alpha male. For a while, Aly spent way too much time surfing the polluted waters of social media.

It's why she hasn't shared her discovery of Fifty-Five with almost anyone. She knows it's a nuanced distinction, between frequencies fifty-five and fifty-two, but she's confident she's found a different whale. *Her* whale. In retrospect, it was dumb to tell Glenn about it; he thinks tracking the fin whale is counterproductive, and made her promise to stop. Or thought he did. Glenn is a hurtful, heartbreaking, two-timing asshole Aly let crawl up under her guard and upend her life—that's what Glenn is.

Power comes back on. Lights glare bright. Live coverage of the fires is interrupted by breaking news of a nightclub shooting, but this flickers mute on the television screen behind Jared when he walks back in with the remote and Aly's note, and because he stops in front of her, Aly can't see the screen crawl that would tell where it's happened.

Does it matter? It seems like there's another shooting every day. La-di-da.

In an envelope on which he's scrawled her name, Vike Maas has left Aly a ticket to the Mickey Madrid show at Club Pandemonium. That might've been fun. Why me? she wonders. Despair burns through her like flames through hillside brush. Leaving only winking embers of melancholy behind.

"You two lovebirds really hit it off," Jared teases, but there's a jealous edge to it.

"I have a boyfriend," Aly reminds him, knowing that, in truth, she doesn't anymore.

"Mickey Madrid?" He nods at the ticket in her hand.

A frown, a shake of the head. "Not really a fan." She puts Vike's proffer back in the envelope and drains her cocktail, letting the ice cube freeze her lips. "Plus, the show started about two hours ago."

"He'll be disappointed."

"He bought the ticket before he even knew I existed," Aly points out.

"Another round?" Jared offers.

Aly doesn't even feel the last one. "Can I take it with me to my pod?" She has a craving to search for her whale again.

"Don't tell the XO," Jared says, setting up a fresh glass on the bar. She watches his hands fly, wonders what it would be like to be touched by them.

"Oh, I won't," Aly assures him.

And avoids his gaze.

* * *

"Ms. Dekker?"

She surfaces from a deepwater doze, head cradled on folded arms, slumped at her station in the Fort Arthur listening room. Sallow dawn light slots through the blinds. The new, crisp, young petty officer from tech support is saying that the XO wants to see her in his office. It takes more than a moment for Aly to wake up and orient herself. The takeaway cocktail Jared made for her last night waits unfinished, diluted now in a sweaty rocks glass on her desk. She shakes off embarrassment for having slept over at work. She remembers ridge fires, new perfume, the little handbag, the butt tattoo, slingshot thong, Glenn's happy huffing—she remembers everything that happened, feels defeated, and small.

It must be her fault, right? The history of their coupling keeps scrolling through her head too fast, scrambled, unhelpful. On her walk down the hallway, she fluffs her hair and smooths her clothes to fashion a more presentable, confident front.

The office door of Lieutenant Commander Glenn Jackson, Fort Arthur's acting XO—a dead-end posting he blames, in his weakest moments, on reverse racism—is gaped open, and she hears him on the phone inside. She can't decide whether she should knock or wait. What is the proper professional etiquette when your boss is your boyfriend whom you've just witnessed romping naked with some tattooed stranger in your apartment, in your bed?

She knocks and walks in.

Glenn, she can tell right away, doesn't know she knows. His face softens into what he must think will express fond concern. He holds up a finger to pause her, then ends his call. "Hey, you." A slanted, low-watt smile. "Everything okay? You never came home."

No guilt in his eyes. Just the usual guile.

Aly makes up something about the fires, the blackout, traffic lights, and work that she needed to wait until power was restored to finish up. She's a coward.

"I heard the whale when I came in and found you asleep," Glenn says, using his chain-of-command voice. Now he's her vice principal, gently chiding. "I thought we both agreed you'd let that go."

They hadn't. Yes, Lieutenant Commander J. Glenn Jackson had instructed her to focus on Navy business and leave the tracking of lovelorn cetaceans to the woke scientists and animal rights activists, but Aly had ignored him.

And now she understands why.

Whale Fifty-Five is searching, she thinks, but not for love. Love is a trap. Love is a lie.

Love burns across your horizons without caution or reason, leaving a charred wasteland of humiliation and regret.

BY DANIEL PYNE

* * *

Since Glenn keeps his service revolver secured in the side drawer of his desk, it's just a matter of waiting for him to go into his staff meeting, then picking the lock with a bobby pin. She's not sure why she does it. Jared is wheeling box cartons of Dos Equis down the hallway when moments later she emerges from the XO's office; they do an awkward pas de deux that obliges her to squeeze past him so close she can smell hazelnut coffee on his breath.

She feels his yearning. Which makes her sad. Is it that he's too handsome? Or not quite handsome enough?

He says something she doesn't register. She has forgotten Jared's last name, if she ever knew it. He gives her the puppy dog look that always annoys her but never fails to take a tug on her heart.

Maybe he still loves me is what she reminds herself, back on Glenn. Maybe he's just been a bad boy. But her chief preoccupation is with the vague, imaginary TikTok that keeps looping through her head, over and over, involving quick cuts of naughty lingerie and scarlet lipstick-whispered nothings that will lead to Glenn's Beretta M9 abruptly nuzzling up against his inevitable erection.

Causing it to go abruptly flaccid.

From there? Who can say?

Bad boys get punished.

All this helps explain Aly's trip to the Little Tart Intimate Apparel Shoppe in Redondo Beach. She's never been here, only driven past. Though she's a long-lapsed Midwestern Methodist, the flimsy outfits on headless, black-velvet window mannequins nevertheless always elicit a prudish blush.

There's a smallish, very fetching young woman with angry, bowl-cut red-and-black hair and the calico-crimsoned complexion of what must be a raging hangover. She's sorting plus-size crotchless panties in the narrow aisle where Aly hopes to find something slutty to wear for the faux-castration ceremonies of her philandering Fort Arthur XO. Brightening when she sees the new customer, the salesgirl asks if Aly needs help, and shoots her a bemused but dubious look when Aly says no, just browsing. Up this close, the girl's eyes are raw and puffy, as if she's been crying off and on for a while.

"Are you allergic to any fabrics?" the girl asks, abandoning her restock to closely follow behind. A knotted Mickey Madrid & All The Things World Tour T-shirt is stretched tight across her chest. Her high-top Chuck Taylors have three-inch soles. A name tag says she's "Bambi," but Aly's pretty sure that's not her name. Aly doesn't want company; she's so self-conscious already she feels dizzy. Disoriented. "I only ask," the girl continues, "because some of these items have been known to cause a nasty rash down below, particularly if you got a Brazilian or, you know, a Hollywood going on."

Aly doesn't want to know about rashes, foreign or domestic. She asks about the girl's T-shirt.

"I was there last night," the girl admits, eyes getting shinier, and she thumbs away a tear. "At Pandemonium. Poor Mickey. Shit was insane. So sad. But. In truth, I didn't see it. Some jerk spilled wine on me. I felt so gross, eventually, that I had to go out in the lobby and buy this shirt and go to the bathroom to clean up, and by the time I came out, everyone was shoving toward the exit, screaming about an active shooter. I mean. Fuck. But." Her mouth turns down.

"Second time for me, too," the girl adds. "Can you believe that? We had a nutcase shoot up my high school back in Texas. I lost, like, three best friends."

All Aly can think to say is "That's sick. I'm so sorry."

"Yeah. America, amirite?"

Aly stops at a budget bin filled with thongs of all colors, tries to imagine herself wearing one.

"Made in China, proceed with caution," the salesgirl advises. "Comfort is beside the point. Basically, just a scrap of lace and some stretchy vaginal floss. You ever worn one before?"

"Yes," Aly lies. Fingers trailing through the tangle of fabric, she goes over her grand scheme again and begins to have doubts. What if she makes a mistake and the gun goes off? Like, for instance, if Glenn tries to disarm her and accidentally trips the trigger?

She thinks about last night's club shooting, then shivers the thought away.

"You got the figure for it. Special occasion?"

"More like a surprise."

"Cool, cool. Boyfriend or husband?" the salesgirl is asking.

"Girlfriend," Aly says for some reason.

Eyebrows lifting ever so slightly, but without missing a beat, the young woman fishes for a satiny teal thong and holds it up, catch of the day. "To match your eyes." Is it a come-on? Made to blush again, Aly's at a loss for words. The young woman grins, takes Aly's elbow, and leads her deeper into the Walmart of lust. "Now, how about some monkey pheromones? Or essential oils?"

Aly's pretty sure she's got everything she needs but welcomes the opportunity to distract herself a little while longer from the dark deed ahead.

* * *

What is she doing?

Trussed up like the cheap chuck roast that her mother always overcooked for Easter dinner, Aly decides the salesgirl at the Little Tart was right: The thong *is* a mistake.

Maybe all of this is.

The day outside has steeped pumpkin-orange. No sun, no clouds, no breeze. An irrational heat. In her little townhouse, chill air shudders through, soured from the dirty filters of an ancient swamp cooler, and only cuts the stubborn heat in fits and starts. Her bare skin pebbles; she shivers on the bed. Her legs are so damp and sticky she keeps them apart, but the gun in her lap rests too heavy and cold as ice.

Crooked rhythms jangle her heart. She's anxious, listening for the hum of Glenn's car pulling into the driveway. No longer sure she can do what she's planned.

For an unhinged moment she even contemplates swerving onto a different road, a dead end, no outlet, do what that shooter at that club did up in Hollywood: pull the pin, eat the gun, take a dirt nap, put herself out of her misery.

That'd be a cruel twist.

Her blood all black, sticky and pooled in the sagging mattress, where he was fucking the contortionist. Like the end of an opera, she'll be dead as a doornail when Glenn walks in, her skin blue, her eyes fixed on the ceiling.

Glenn loves those kinds of movies.

She's not, though. In misery. If she's being honest.

That's the actual problem here.

She's hurt, yeah. Ashamed. Love is a crapshoot, and Aly keeps throwing snake eyes. Stooping to the lamest, cheapest clichés.

What does that even mean, anyway, dead doornail?

A car door bangs shut out front, and she freezes, waiting for the key she gave him to rattle in the dead bolt. Then a second car door shuts. Followed by the familiar chirp of her neighbor's Prius alarm. Not Glenn. Not yet.

And, yes, under this, under everything, as if indelible, and insistent, she thinks, there's that steady fifty-five hertz keening growl and click of a solitary fin whale whose song isn't some plaintive, searching query.

No. It's a warning, a Siren's call.

An idling V-8 rumbles up outside; there's a coy squeak of shocks, the sibilant tread of tires on the driveway. Engine ticking when the Camaro falls quiet. Glenn is home.

Her heart skips.

She can't do it. He can't find her here.

Key in the dead bolt, the front door wheezing open. She scrambles off the bed, begins to fumble into her clothes.

"Hullo? Aly?"

She hears him come up the stairs, and when he walks into the room, her shirt is still open and unbuttoned, and her pants are only halfway to her hips. From the leer in his look, he approves. Grins, toothy.

"The hell's going on in here, girlie mine? And how can I help?"

His playful eyes lower to her breasts, predictably headed farther south, but swerve to land on the service revolver on the bed, and now they cloud over. Mortified, Aly picks the gun up. Feels the feral power of its dark promise. She shivers again, but not from the cold.

A strange silence falls between them. As if the known world has collapsed into her bedroom and is holding its breath.

"Is that mine?" Glenn asks.

"Yeah," Aly admits.

He's every bit as handsome as she remembers. She smells perfume on him, faint, expensive, not hers. His forgotten smile is static, frozen on his face. A relic from another realm.

He knows she knows; it doesn't seem to faze him.

And for some reason, without really meaning to, without giving it a second thought—though she understands that, in some hazy repentant future, lying awake at night (in prison? death row?) she might puzzle over it for a long, long time and never find the answer—Aly grips, regrips, and lifts the gun the way Glenn taught her at the range. One purposeful, arcing motion.

As if from a great distance, boundless oceans of loss and recrimination roiling between here and there, she waits for a braver version of herself to squeeze the trigger and empty a whole clip into the center of her ex-boyfriend's chest.

www.ingramcontent.com/pod-product-compliance
Lightning Source LLC
LaVergne TN
LVHW032009070526
838202LV00059B/6357